THE China TATE SERIES
THE SECRET IN THE KITCHEN

LISSA HALLS JOHNSON

PUBLISHING

Colorado Springs, Colorado

For Amber Mello
My adopted daughter.
May your hurts for today
be your strength for tomorrow.

With special thanks to Jacob Roebuck—
who ran around the kitchen helping
me brainstorm how one could get
locked inside a walk-in refrigerator.

THE SECRET IN THE KITCHEN

Copyright © 1994 by Lissa Halls Johnson.
All rights reserved. International copyright secured.

Library of Congress Cataloging-in-Publication Data
Johnson, Lissa Halls, 1955–
    The secret in the kitchen / Lissa Halls Johnson.
        p.   cm.
    Summary: While trying to keep the dog she and Deedee rescued hidden, China is caught up in some mysterious occurrences at Camp Crazy Bear.
    ISBN 1-56179-282-9
    [1. Camps—Fiction. 2. Christian life—Fiction. 3. Dogs—Fiction.] I. Title.
PZ8.J464Se   1994
[Fic]—dc20
                                    94-16858
                                         CIP
                                          AC

Published by Focus on the Family Publishing,
Colorado Springs, Colorado 80995.
Distributed by Word Books, Dallas, Texas.

The author is represented by the literary agency of Alive Communications, P.O. Box 49068, Colorado Springs, CO 80920.

This is a work of fiction, and any resemblance between the characters in this book and real persons is coincidental.

Editor: Deena Davis
Cover Design: Jim Lebbad
Cover Illustration: Paul Casale

Printed in the United States of America
94 95 96 97 98 99 / 10 9 8 7 6 5 4 3 2 1

CHAPTER ONE

CHINA TATE AND DEEDEE KIERSEY STOOD at the edge of an oblong pool of mud covered with a layer of putrid water. Deedee wrinkled her nose. "How can Kemper lovingly call this glamour goo?"

"What's the problem?" China asked, gingerly holding up the baggy white T-shirt Deedee's father, the director of Camp Crazy Bear, had donated for the occasion. "Is it that he calls it glamour goo or the fact that he adores it?"

"It's his undying love affair with it that bugs me." Deedee let her T-shirt dangle around her knobby knees.

"Face it. Kemper, like all youth directors, has a love affair with anything bizarre or nuts."

The silky mud oozed between China's toes as she stood at the edge surveying the pit. It was about 40 feet long and 20 feet wide. The shady end was virtually unusable, since it ended at the edge of some scrub brush. Other than a rock that had probably tumbled from the brush, the borders of the pit were smooth.

Most of it cooked in the sun. "What're we doing this for, Deedee? I forgot."

"To have fun, and to test out next week's high school camp games for Kemper. Remember?"

China shook her long, tawny hair. "No, I think I've forgotten. Or I was insane when I said yes. Or maybe I didn't say yes. Maybe you conned me into this. Dang, this stuff stinks!"

Deedee pulled her long red curls into a fluorescent green scrunchie. "Want one? I brought the ugly ones so it doesn't matter if they get ruined."

China took the fluorescent pink-with-black-polka-dot scrunchie from Deedee's hand. As she wrapped it around her straight hair, they took a few more sloshing steps. Suddenly, Deedee's slender hand motioned in the air. "Stop!"

China froze, looking at Deedee's solemn face, prepared for the worst.

"Drop!" Deedee commanded, falling into the muddy water.

China crossed her arms defiantly. "Are you nuts?"

Deedee jerked upright, her green eyes blazing. "Drop!" She punctuated her command with a flying clump of mud. China dropped, the musty water running down her back.

"Roll!" Deedee shrieked, her maniacal laughter echoing off the mountain walls.

Both girls rolled over and over, covering themselves with the stinky, gray mud. China pinned Deedee to the soupy ground, scooped a handful of mud, and happily rubbed it through Deedee's gorgeous hair.

"Stop it, you freak!" Deedee shouted, grabbing mud and smearing it on China's face.

China screamed. Letting go of Deedee, she tried to wash off her face in the gritty water, but only succeeded in getting the smelly stuff up her nose. She snorted and gray gunk spewed out.

"Gross, China!"

China stopped, the whites of her eyes contrasting with her face. "What am I supposed to do?"

Deedee stood up and sloshed to the side of the pit where she grabbed an inner tube. "What you are supposed to do, China, is go to work. One of Kemper's games is 'Steal the Bacon.' We have to see if it's at all possible to wrestle for this thing and not kill each other in the process."

"And if we do kill each other, when will they find the bodies?"

"Tuesday, when the kids come to play in the mud pit."

"You really think Kemper's going to get a couple hundred kids to play in this disgusting stuff?"

"He got us to do it, didn't he? Come on. Let's try the game. It might be fun."

"Fine. You'll get killed, and I'll win the bacon." China stood with her feet spread apart, her knees springy. She swayed back and forth snarling, her arms curved like an ape's.

"Hah!" Deedee slapped the tube down on the water between them. "One, two, THREE!"

Both girls grabbed the tube and began pulling. Their slimy hands made it difficult to get a good grip. China linked her arm through the tube and yanked. It only took two good pulls before she fell on her butt, having dislodged Deedee's grip from the other side. Deedee grabbed the tube again while China struggled to regain her footing. Once on her feet, she gave one swift yank, pulling Deedee flat on her face, and sprinted toward the opposite bank.

"I won!" she shouted, jumping up and down. "I won!"

A bedraggled Deedee stood in the center of the pit, gray water dripping everywhere. Her T-shirt had grown two inches longer. "Big deal. You have stronger muscles than me. And, you weigh much more than me."

China charged and rammed Deedee with the inner tube, knocking her back in the water.

"Okay! Okay! Uncle! I give up! You win."

China strutted around, the tube hanging from her arm. "I'm beginning to like this," she said, then tossed the inner tube outside the pit. "What's next?"

"The Washing Machine. You know, the one where you put your forehead on top of a stick or baseball bat, run around 10 times like a washer on the spin cycle, then run back to your team."

"I'm ready." China took the 3-foot stick and plunged it into the ground at the edge of the pit. With her forehead on the top, she began to walk in circles.

"Faster!" encouraged Deedee. "Remember, this one is done for time."

"This isn't bad," China said, moving around the stick.

"Five, six, seven," Deedee counted.

"Oh, dear," China moaned, "the world is moving with me now. How does the ground slant like that?"

"Nine, keep going, 10! Okay, run!"

China let go of the stick and promptly fell in the water. She tried to stand and run, but some invisible force held her, dragging her to the right.

"Run straight, China, or you'll end up at the wrong team!"

"I can't," China called back. "I'm being led in this direction! It must be God's will!" She stumbled in slow motion, her body leaning, until she finally landed in the mud.

"You are so weird!" Deedee giggled.

China rolled onto her back, her arms and legs splayed. "I'm done! I can't go any more! This game gets a zero."

"No, it doesn't. It gets the go-ahead. It's hysterical to watch."

"Ha, ha, ha," China monotoned. "Very funny."

Deedee squeezed the water from the bottom of her T-shirt and moved toward China. "Here, let me help you." She held out her hand and China took it. China gave one swift yank and Deedee was in the water, too. "I'll get you, my pretty," Deedee cackled, "and your little dog, too!"

Mud flew, water splashed, shrieks filled the canyon. They wrestled around, then China chased Deedee to the shady part of the pit. Deedee's hand flew up in the air again. "Stop!" she demanded.

China shook her head. "Not again." She pushed around Deedee and glanced toward her feet. Her heart started beating wildly. The dizziness came back. "What is it?"

"Is it real?" Deedee asked.

"I . . . I . . . don't know. When we first got here I thought it was a rock. It looks kind of fake. Like a crumpled clay statue."

"Touch it."

China crouched low beside the gray lump. Whatever it was had lots of mud stuck in the fur. Whatever it was didn't move.

Deedee crouched next to her. "Is it alive?"

Both girls watched the lump carefully. China reached out and gently touched it. Her hand jerked back, her face twisted. "It's gooey and squishy."

"Statues aren't gooey."

China glared at Deedee. "No, duh."

"Sorry."

China again reached out, this time leaving her fingers lightly on the "rock." "It's breathing," she reported.

Deedee kept her hands clasped in her lap. "What'll we do?"

"Thank God Kemper thought to put showers in.

Let's wash it off."

"Thanks, God," Deedee whispered.

China began stroking the creature. The dried mud made it look unreal. Like a statue of a small, blackish-gray lamb. When the creature didn't bite, she shoved her hands underneath and waited. No response. "I think it's a dog."

Deedee nodded. "I'll go turn on the shower." She ran up the hill and was ready for China as soon as she reached the cement pad. Eight shower heads stuck on pipes jutting out of the ground were placed in a rectangle on the cement. One twist of a knob, and water poured out of all the shower heads at once.

China placed her small bundle on the warm cement. As the water poured down on them both, she stroked the matted fur, loosening the mud clumps. Periodically, she wiped her own face of the dripping water. She washed the mud from the dog's eyes and was careful to get the mud out of its ears without more going inside.

"It's all skin and bones," she wailed to Deedee. The more mud she washed off, the more her own tears added to the water spray.

Deedee stayed at the shower control and nodded. "Is it alive?"

"Barely," China whispered, as though talking loud might suck the last bit of breath from the dog. "We've got to get it to a vet."

"There isn't one anywhere around here."

"Can't we have your dad take us?"

Deedee shook her head. "Dad's allergic to dogs. Besides, what would the vet do? Take it to the pound? I've seen animals that look better than this taken to the pound and put to sleep. And I think there's some rule about no animals on the grounds except the wild ones that naturally live here."

"Well, I'm not about to let this one die because of a stupid rule."

Deedee nodded slowly. "I don't make the rules, China . . ."

"And I don't usually break them. But I'll fight you on this one, Deedee," China snapped.

"Hey! Don't come all unglued on me. I'm on your side."

China's shoulders relaxed. She gently rubbed the small dog's bony head. "I'm sorry. I'm just so scared for this little guy. What're we going to do?"

Deedee moved underneath one of the shower heads. She gently tugged on the scrunchie, now an indiscernible color, until it released its hold on her mop of red curls. She stood with her back to the pipe, and moved her hair around to get rid of most of the mud. China sat on the ground, cradling the small dog in her lap. Its tail gave a feeble twitch. "We could hide it," she suggested.

Deedee took her head out from under the water. "What?"

"Do you know where we could hide him?"

Deedee went back to working on her muddy hair. She faced the water, letting it wash off her face. "The old maintenance shack. It hasn't been used for a couple years. It's disgusting, but pretty well hidden."

"Let's do it."

China struggled to her feet, trying to keep her balance while holding the dog close to her body. Deedee cranked the water spigot off. "Where will we get food?"

"We'll talk to Magda."

"But she'll tell Daddy what we're up to."

"I'll think of something."

"Don't lie, China."

China stopped, adjusting the dog to a more comfortable position. "I won't lie, Deedee, I promise. Shoot. For a kid who says she's sick of being spoon-fed all this Christian stuff, you sure do want to stick to the rules."

Deedee shrugged. "I fluctuate. Maybe I've heard it all for so long that I couldn't be bad if I wanted."

"Yeah, I know how you feel. Every time I try to do something wrong, my MK* upbringing always wins."

Deedee kicked a rock, the dust turning to mud as it clung to her shoes. She grinned slyly, thinking of what happened with Heather "The queen" Hamilton the week before. "It doesn't always win, China."

China looked at Deedee. "What are you . . . ?"

"Sliced Heather on toast?"**

China rolled her eyes. "Gee, I thought when God forgives you of something you can leave it behind."

Deedee laughed. "Maybe you could if it wasn't such a humdinger."

China laughed with her. "Yeah, yeah."

Deedee stopped on the path. "Shhh! I think I hear someone coming."

---

*Missionary Kid.

**"Sliced Heather on toast" is a threat China made in Book 1 of the Camp Crazy Bear Series.

CHAPTER TWO

"**Y**OU HIDE OVER THERE," Deedee pointed to a small group of trees fronted by scrub brush.

China ducked out of sight just as Kemper came into view. "Yo! Deedee!" His eyes quickly traveled over her clothing. "I see you tried out the mud pit. What's the verdict? Where's China? Did you drown her in the mud? You think the kids will like it?"

"I didn't drown her, she drowned herself." Deedee pulled damp hair away from her forehead. "China swore she hated it. But she loved it, I can tell."

"You think they'll go for it?" Kemper removed a pencil from a clump of wiry, black hair bushed over his ear, then stuck it back again.

Deedee smiled, nodding eagerly. "The stench is a killer, though."

"Yeah, we've thought about that. I think we're going to add chlorine. That should kill the stench and any amoebas trying to use our hole for a breeding ground."

Deedee glanced backwards down the path. "I thought China was coming right up behind me. I guess I'd better go find her."

Kemper nodded. "I could use the help of you girls this week with the games. Actually, every week if you're interested. You can be the guinea pigs who show them how it works."

"I'll ask China and we'll let you know."

"Keep the faith!" Kemper said. He saluted the air with his huge hand and lumbered up the path.

When he was out of hearing, China muttered through the bushes, "If I were new around here I'd think it was a bear coming through the trees. I've never heard someone walk so loud in the forest before."

"He'd make a terrible Indian," Deedee agreed. "Let's go."

The maintenance shed had turned into a hotel for spiders and beetles. Mice had been there at one time, but probably left for more rewarding spots, like the cabins where kids brought a smorgasbord of food to munch on.

China sat where no one could see her, cooing to the drying bundle on her lap. She stroked his head and body, gently loosening the last bits of mud. A few times, the little guy licked her hand.

Deedee swept out the shack, then went to find some old towels and blankets from the lost-and-never-found bin in housekeeping and made a soft bed for the dog. She sat cross-legged next to China.

"You've been hogging him long enough. It's my turn. You can find the water and food."

China stood, brushing off the seat of her pants, hesitating. "But . . ."

"Go. You're not being fair."

"I have to shower and change before I go to the kitchen. Magda would chase me with that huge wooden spoon of hers if I dared come anywhere near her precious kitchen looking like this."

"So go home and change." Deedee paused to put her massive hair back in the now-gray scrunchie.

"Won't your mom wonder why you aren't with me?"

"No. She's used to me being dirty. When you grow up in the mountains, dirt is no big deal. You city folk can't stand one ounce of dirt clinging to your bodies."

China opened her mouth to protest. But it was true. Her skin itched from the dried mud the shower hadn't washed off. Her hair stunk like the pit. Now that she thought about it, cleaning up wouldn't take her away from the dog that long. Besides, he needed food and water more than anything.

Thirty minutes later, China charged into the Eela-puash kitchen door almost running into a tall, dark blond, very muscular, very homely male. He carried a large foil-covered pan of something with industrial strength hot pads protecting each hand. A blue and gold Dodger cap sat on his head. "Whoa, girl! Hot stuff coming through! Lasagna." He kept moving, China watching him every step of the way. Not too many guys her age had bodies that moved like that. A well-trained machine. Oiled. Smooth. Except . . . she tilted her head. He limped, just a bit. His left arm not quite so muscular. *Too bad he's got a fatal case of the uglies.*

"Well, China honey!" came a rippling voice behind her. Magda, the high school camp cook, wrapped her fleshy arms around China, who got lost in the layers of chins and bosoms. "It's been almost 24 hours since I've seen you, girl. Don't be such a stranger." She released China and gestured behind her. "This here's another new worker. Rick Marshall."

China turned around to see the Lasagna Man returning from his journey. His left hand curled inward. She wasn't sure if he did it on purpose or not.

"And this here's China Jasmine Tate. She works the dinner shift Monday through Friday. Hard worker, good kid."

"Magda!" China protested. She held out her hand to Rick, who took it and stared into her eyes as he slowly lifted her hand to his mouth and lightly kissed the back. "China Jasmine Tate, I'm awfully pleased to meet you."

China looked into his eyes. Eyes to get lost in. Eyes that drew her away from the face that had no chin and the nose that could almost support a ski slope. His eyes beckoned her to come closer, even though alarms in her head told her to back away. His eyes seemed open, yet . . . there was something behind them she couldn't figure out. A lame "Yeah" was all she managed to say.

Magda playfully whacked his arm. "That Rick," she said to both of them. "Always the lady's man. He can charm a brick wall, he can."

I doubt that, though.

Rick just looked at China and smiled. A killer smile. A smile that totally wiped out all memory of the rest of his imperfections. "I think we'll enjoy working together."

China tried to smile. But once you've melted, it's difficult to do anything but just lie there in a puddle. *Why are you in a puddle, China? He's not cute. He's too old. He's . . . well, he not only has some kind of deformity, he's downright painful to look at.*

Magda put her arm around China, directing her toward the stainless steel preparation table. "Come over here and tell me what's on your mind while I roll and cut biscuits."

China leaned on the prep table, reached over, and popped a stray piece of dough into her mouth. "You make the best biscuits, Magda."

"Don't butter me up, China honey. I know something's on your mind. You never could hide those pain-filled eyes from me."

Rick's voice came bellowing out from the dish-washing area on the other side of the wall. "Well! You can't get to Heaven!" (then, in a tiny, silly, girly voice) "No, you can't get to Heaven!"

"On roller skates!" ("On roller skates!")

Magda wagged her head and said with affection, "Don't mind him. He's a little nuts."

"Well," China began, breathing deeply. She tried to think quickly what she could say that would not be a lie but would get her what she wanted. "Deedee and I went to the mud pit."

"You got into a fight?"

"No . . . it's what we saw."

Magda stopped cutting to look at China.

"We saw tracks to the mud pit. I . . . I think something is hurt. Some small animal." She started talking faster as the ideas popped into her head. "Deedee and I figured that the animal must be hurt to be coming to look for water in a mud pit rather than the creek. And so we thought maybe you could give us an old bowl that we could fill with fresh water and put in the bushes by the mud pit. Then the little critter wouldn't have to die from lack of water."

Magda went back to rolling and cutting, lifting and putting discs of dough onto industrial baking trays. Her mouth opened to speak.

China kept going. "And, I thought maybe if the little critter was hurt enough to have to go to the mud pit for water, then it might be starving, too. And if it's sick enough, maybe we should set food out for it so it can eat."

Magda shook her head. "It's far too dangerous to put food out. The bears will come into camp. That's happened before and we certainly don't want it to happen again. Whew! What a mess!"

"But . . . we aren't trying to feed bears."

"No, but that's what you would end up feeding. Besides, it's very dangerous to teach wild animals to become dependent on humans for food. God made them with their own specific dietary needs. We don't want them getting used to goodies they shouldn't have, now do we? They might end up looking like me!" Magda patted a floury hand on her stomach, chuckling at herself.

China shifted her weight back and forth. She tried to think of an alternate plan. Rick's silly singing didn't help. He'd started to sing what he wanted in a nanny. That totally interrupted her thinking process, making her think of Mary Poppins instead of how to get food for the dog. Rick kept walking by carrying things. He'd skip or prance or do something else that would make them smile.

Magda leaned over, putting a soft, floured hand on China's arm. "Sometimes it's better to let the sick creatures die. It's God's . . ."

"No! I won't let it die." Tears came to China's eyes as she thought about the little dog dying simply because he was too sick to get his own food and water.

Magda stared at China. "Okay, China honey. I'll let you take an old bowl. But no food. That's just too dangerous."

China mumbled her thanks and followed Magda to

the back recesses of the kitchen. "Excuse me, John," Magda said as she squeezed her bulk past him. To China she said, "You know John don't you?"

John gave China a crooked grin. "So the scholarship kid is back."

"For the summer," China added. "If you can stand me."

John shrugged his shoulders. "Makes no difference to me."

Magda returned with an old steel bowl that had obviously seen better days. Magda excused herself again, handed the bowl to China, and went back to her biscuits. China moved slowly to the backdoor. She slipped out then turned, walking right into Rick again.

"Making this a habit, are we?" he asked playfully.

"I'm sorry. I'm just upset."

"I heard."

"How could you hear over the singing?"

"Practice." He brought his left hand out from behind his back. In its clutch was a plastic bag full of food. "Here."

China's mouth dropped open. She took the bag and looked inside. Chunks of meat. Leftover scrambled egg. Biscuits.

Rick leaned over and said in a low tone. "I know you found a sick animal. Your story didn't fool me any. You tell me what kind of scraps you need, and I'll try to get them for you."

"Thanks so much!" China whispered.

Rick grabbed her wrist. China winced at the sudden pain and tried to pull away, but his grip tightened. He looked at her hard. "You owe me one, sweetheart." He paused, pulling her closer. "And don't forget it." He dropped her wrist and smiled happily.

China blinked twice, her brain trying to sort out the conflicting images. "Yeah," she said, trying to laugh. "Uh, yeah, sure."

"I'd like to see what you found. I love animals."

"Okay. Maybe. If it lives."

"It will live as long as someone as wonderful as you is caring for it." Rick grabbed the bowl from her hand and popped it on top of her head like a hat. "Smile, China Jasmine Tate! You've got a gorgeous one."

She turned to walk away. The bowl on her head somehow made her feel stupid rather than playful. She heard the screen door close and her whole body seemed to relax. She took the bowl off her head and ran all the way to the maintenance shed.

Deedee looked up at China, her hand stroking the sleeping dog. "How'd you do?"

China answered by setting down the bowl of water and taking some scrambled eggs from the bag. She held the eggs to the dog's nose. He sniffed and then his little pink tongue came out and ate them. Deedee opened her mouth in surprise, her eyebrows raised high on her forehead. "How'd you con all that food out of Magda?" her eyes accused. "Did you lie to her?"

"Magda didn't give us the food. Rick did."

She positioned the water closer to the dog. He struggled to get up on shaky forelegs high enough to be able to drink. Too weak to hold his weight, his legs collapsed, his nose smacking the edge of the bowl.

"Rick? Who's Rick?"

China scooped water out with her hand, holding it under the dog's muzzle. He eagerly lapped it.

"Some new guy who works there." China raised her eyebrows and gave an evil grin. "A guy . . ." she breathed on her nails and polished them on her shirt, "who greeted me by kissing my hand."

"What? You're joking?"

China shook her head.

"You lucky bum. All I ever get are these older lifeguards who breeze in and out of the boat shack about once a decade. I could be invisible for all they care. Except when they want to try scaring me with rubber snakes and beetles."

China shrugged. "I don't know if I'm so lucky."

"Why?

"Actually he's kind of, well, deformed or something. He limps and his left hand looks almost like a claw. He's not very cute or anything . . ."

"China!" Deedee said. "I can't believe you'd say that, much less not like him because of how he looks. Since when is cute important?"

"Since always. *You* don't pay any attention to guys unless they're cute."

"Maybe I don't want to go out with someone who isn't cute. But I don't judge his whole character on what he looks like."

"Well, there's also something behind his eyes. I don't trust someone whose eyes say they're hiding something."

"Oh, don't give me that, China. You can't tell a person by his eyes."

"Sure you can. My dad says he can tell anyone's motives by watching their eyes. That's why he's such a good missionary to the village Indians. He may not understand their dialect, but he can tell when he's in danger, talking to the person in charge, or whatever. He says anyone can learn how."

"Fine. You learn and I'll keep trusting people in my own way."

Deedee tried to give the dog a lump of hamburger. It went into the pink mouth and fell out again. "I wonder if we need something more mushy for him."

China nodded. "If I can get up enough nerve, I'll ask Rick." She focused her attention on the dog, but her mind kept going back to Rick. *Rick the sweet, fun person; Rick who leaned more toward strange-looking than cute. And what about the Rick who hurt her wrist?* She shook the yucky thoughts from her head, telling herself she should have a better attitude. Besides, she probably misunderstood his way of making a joke. Everyone had different ways of joking to make you feel at ease. He obviously had many sides to his humor. Just because she didn't like one way he played a joke didn't mean she should think anything bad about him.

"He's really funny," China said suddenly, trying to make Deedee see she really wasn't shallow.

"Rick?"

"Yeah. If it weren't for his eyes, I'd say he could be one of us." *But I hope he won't be. I might be embarrassed if someone saw me with him.*

"Great," Deedee said sarcastically, "we need another loony person at this camp."

The new week's campers began to arrive during the late afternoon. The girls could hear their shouts and calls echoing, a signal to Deedee it was time to report to her job at the registration kiosk. When she returned two hours later, China was waiting for her in front of the maintenance shack. "He's sleeping," China told her.

"Ready for dinner?" Deedee asked.

"Yep." China stood to follow her. "Did anyone comment on your gorgeous looks and lovely perfume?"

Deedee pushed up on her hair, moving about like a snotty model. "Of course. I told them in a couple of days they too would be lucky enough to look and smell like me."

At dinner, Deedee's family piled taco salad onto their plates. Deedee tucked her now-clean hair behind her ears and plopped her chin on her hand. "Daddy."

Mr. Kiersey popped a forkful of salad into his mouth. "Hmm?"

"Can China and I sleep out tonight?"

"Where?"

"In the old maintenance shed."

China's eyes grew wide. She kicked Deedee under the table. Another kick answered hers.

"I wanna go, I wanna go," said Deedee's five-year-old sister, Eve, jumping up and down in her seat.

"Go?" chirped two-year-old Anna. She quickly stuck her thumb in her mouth as if to stop the word.

"You can't go," 11-year-old Adam growled at Eve. "You're just a baby."

"Am not!"

Adam flicked a corn chip at her with his fork. No one but China saw. Eve stuck her tongue out at him.

"Why would you want to sleep in that old, awful thing?" Diana, Deedee's mom asked.

Deedee finished chewing. "We cleaned it up this afternoon. It isn't so bad. It's kind of like having our own cabin."

Mr. Kiersey put his fork down, pushing his fingers together like spiders doing push-ups. China smiled to herself. That meant he was thinking.

"I think Joseph and I should go," Adam said with authority.

"You and Joseph can set up the tent in the backyard near the creek," Diana suggested.

Nine-year-old Joseph, always preferring to

communicate with gestures rather than words, looked at his big brother and nodded vigorously.

"Cool!" Adam said, wolfing down an especially large bite.

"You know," Mr. Kiersey said, again lifting his fork. "I don't see any reason why not. Rain's not expected. If you don't mind the night bugs crawling on you, I sure don't."

"Dave!" Diana scolded.

"Bugs?" asked Eve. "I don't wanna sleep with bugs."

Deedee smiled at her. "Oh, well, I guess you shouldn't go then."

"Bugs," Anna said, milk spewing out with the word.

CHAPTER THREE

CHINA LEFT DEEDEE at the maintenance shack to figure out how they'd fit two sleeping bags and a dog in the tiny wood shelter. She carried the mostly untouched bag of food to a bear-proof trash can and dropped it in.

Inside the kitchen, Rick swept around the floor as if he were some highly energetic ballroom dancer. "Put that over there! Thank you, John! Carolyn, don't dribble the lasagna cheese across the warmer. It sticks. China! What can I do for you?"

China looked around the kitchen. "Where's Magda?"

"Sick." He did a little soft-shoe shuffle and ended with a stomp, his arms outstretched.

"Sick? She seemed fine this afternoon."

"It came on her all of a sudden. She must have gotten hit by the proverbial dump truck."

China wrinkled her brow. "You seem awfully happy about it."

Rick shrugged his shoulders. "John! No! The lasagna

pans have to go in the presoak sink." He turned back to China. "Not happy necessarily, but when God opens a door of opportunity, I fly through it."

"That's mean!"

"Do you think so? I'm sure Magda's okay and isn't permanently damaged."

China eyed him carefully. His eyes looked sincere, but with that same indistinguishable shadow lurking in the background. "What opportunity are you talking about?"

"Well, all my life I've wanted the chance to prove I can run a kitchen and run it well. Too many times I've gotten the old boot for some stupid thing or other that wasn't my fault. It always happened before I had my big chance. I've always suspected it was because of my hand and my limp. It seems odd that few people are willing to look past the outside package to the hard worker inside."

Rick looked at her as if trying to see what type of person she was. She turned her head so he couldn't see her eyes. "Well!" he continued, "No one was quite willing to believe that someone who looked like me could possibly have a brain and talent. So, China Jasmine, our beloved Magda's going to give me that chance. And you are going to be my star player."

John stuck his head around the corner. "And what about me? Am I chopped fish?"

"The saying is 'chopped liver,' John—which you will be if you don't get that bread baked."

"Don't I get any recognition for this?" John persisted.

"Sure, sure," Rick said with a wave of his good hand. "But you aren't as pretty as China."

"Fine," John said, throwing a wadded up towel at them.

Rick laughed, then hopped up to sit on the preparation table and took both of China's hands in his. Her whole body cringed again at the touch of his crippled hand. "I hear you're the best worker Magda's got," Rick told her. "You'll do anything to make sure the job gets done. So I'm more than proud to have you on my team."

China frowned, not liking the idea that this stranger was to be in charge. She pulled gently, trying to release her hands, but Rick didn't let go. "I feel uncomfortable," she said quietly.

Rick dropped her hands. "Oh. Sorry. I didn't mean anything by it." He clapped his hands, then wrung them together as if he rubbed gobs of hand lotion into them. "So! Are you going to be part of the team?"

"Sure, but maybe Magda will be back tomorrow."

"I don't think so. She looked pretty bad."

China shifted from one foot to the other. She shoved her hands into the back pockets of her jeans. "I'd better go see her."

"She'd be happy to see you. Hey, you could ask her what she wants to eat tomorrow. I'll make her whatever she wants."

"That's nice." China somehow felt she was lying. Magda being sick wasn't nice at all. And China didn't know if she wanted to be on Rick's team or not.

Rick glanced around. When he didn't see anyone, he leaned over and whispered. "You're a very pretty girl. Has anyone ever told you that?"

China felt her face grow hot. She looked into Rick's eyes and saw they were sincere. Beckoning. Encouraging her to come close. "Uh, I don't think so."

"Shame! Oh! We should get you more food for that little animal of yours."

China nodded. Her throat felt like it had been glued shut.

"More meat?"

She shook her head and cleared her throat. "I think something real mushy. Oatmeal. Or soup."

"Wow. We're talking a real sick animal then. How about oatmeal made with soup broth?"

China nodded enthusiastically.

"I'll even put some in a thermos for later." Rick's voice grew soft. "I don't want this animal to die either."

His softness melted her heart. "It's a dog," she told him.

His shoulders drooped. He leaned forward, resting his hands on the table. "What kind?"

"I don't know. Some kind of small mutt. Part poodle, I think."

His eyes brimmed with tears. "I had a poodle growing up. Dumb-looking dogs. Everyone made fun of mine. Said it was a sissy dog. But he was my best friend." His eyes looked beyond her, seeing into the past. His voice dropped so low she almost didn't hear what he said. "My only friend until . . ." He shook his head. "Never mind."

China didn't know what to say, so she nodded, hoping her own eyes would convey the understanding she felt.

Rick clapped his hands and jumped from the table, startling China. "I'll grind up some meat real fine and mix it with the mush. Go see Magda. When you get back, I'll have it ready."

China headed for the maintenance shack, ignoring the milling students, not even seeing them. Instead, she saw images of a lonely little boy named Rick, taunted and ridiculed because he had a dog that wasn't the kind a boy should have. And because he limped a little and had a hand that wasn't like everyone else's. Who thought up these rules anyway? Who decided what was acceptable? She felt her face grow hot. *I'm no better than the rest of them.*

She also worried about Magda. Rick made it sound like she was really sick. She probably didn't have the stomach flu if he thought she could eat. She pushed open the rotting, wooden shed door. "Deedee?" she whispered. "How's the little guy?"

"Weak, but I think he's starting to come around a little."

China went to the pup and stroked his body. She

gently massaged his legs and body. His tail lifted and fell a couple of times. He turned his head to look at her. China buried her face in his neck and whispered to him. Then she sat up and said to Deedee, "Do you think we can leave him for a little while? Magda's sick."

"He's too weak to run away. Let's go take care of Magda."

They made the dog comfortable, then walked out into the cool evening air. A lot of the camp kids looked lost and alone. A few walked in twos or groups. The groups were fairly boisterous. "Was it only a week ago I was one of them?" China asked incredulously.

"A lifetime can happen in a week at camp," Deedee said solemnly.

"I wouldn't have believed it if I hadn't lived it," China said. "Thanks for letting me stay the summer."

"Hey, don't give me the credit. Remember, it was my mom who arranged it."

Their feet scuffled through the dirt, occasionally hindered by small rocks. China's white tennis shoes had long since turned a dusty brown. Deedee's ever-present hiking boots left waffle prints behind.

China knocked softly on Magda's door. "Magda? It's China and Deedee. Do you want company?"

"Yes" came a voice that was decidedly not the Magda that either girl knew.

They opened the door and stepped in. The cabin was one room, not counting the bathroom positioned off to one side. One end of the room had an old sofa with a worn bedspread tossed over it. An oval braided rug separated the sofa from the rocking chair and a tall bookshelf filled with books and knickknacks. A massive overstuffed chair sat to one side, also facing the sofa. On the other end of the room an antique, wrought-iron single bed sat in the corner with a very large lump on top of it. A dresser stood next to the bed, covered with tissues, a Bible, some pens, and a spiral notebook.

"Hi, girls," rasped Magda.

China went to the bed first and reached out to stroke Magda's forehead. "What's wrong?"

Deedee stood behind China and picked up Magda's hand, gently patting it.

"I don't know. I felt fine this morning and part of the afternoon. But about 3:00, I started to feel very strange. Heavy." She stared at the girls. "I know, I should have felt heavy a long time before this."

China tried not to smile. She sensed Deedee move suddenly.

"Go ahead, laugh. I'd be stupid if I pretended I wasn't fat."

The girls chuckled. "I'm glad you're still able to laugh," Deedee said brightly.

"That's about all I can do. My head feels like someone split it open with an ax."

China continued to stroke Magda's forehead, pushing tendrils of salt-and-pepper hair away from her face. She looked so much older, so frail in bed like this.

"Rick sent me to find out what you want to eat tomorrow."

"What a sweetheart. Was he doing okay?"

"A little crazy maybe . . ."

"That's Rick. Always a little crazy." Magda's face suddenly contorted and she moaned. She writhed away from the girls, pulling her hand from Deedee's. "I feel so awful. I've never felt like this before."

Deedee's green eyes became very intense. "Do you want me to tell Daddy to get a doctor?"

"No. The nurse has seen me. I'm sure it's just some flu bug. I'll be out of here in no time."

The girls took her menu order and left after putting a cool washcloth on her forehead. They stopped by the kitchen to give Rick the list of food.

Rick smiled at Deedee. "So! You're the infamous Director's Daughter. D.D. Pleased to meet you!" He shook her hand cordially, then turned a special smile to China. "And here is that wonderful person, that pretty, cute, Florence Nightingale of the animal kingdom. I salute you . . ." he took her hand and kissed it again. China blushed, and Deedee put her hand over her mouth to stifle a laugh.

"Hey, you two," Rick continued. "I made some dynamite stuff. Here," he said, dipping a spoon into a simmering pot. "Taste it."

Deedee wrinkled her nose. "I don't think so."

China smiled, pretending to play up to him. "You're a dear to offer, but I think I'll pass."

Rick shrugged. "Have it your way," he said, then he stuck the spoon in his own mouth. "Umm, umm. Best potion I ever made."

He poured most of the slop into a thermos and gave it to China. Then he put the rest into a steel bowl and handed it to Deedee. "I stayed late just for you ladies and your mongrel." His smile said he was pleased to do it, but his eyes still had that shadow China had seen earlier.

"And are we ever grateful!" Deedee said, returning his smile. "We're in your debt."

Rick bowed. "You certainly are."

As they turned to leave, Rick padlocked the walk-in freezer and refrigerator doors, then flicked off the kitchen light and locked the door behind them. "I'll see you two bright and early so you can take breakfast to Magda!" Then he turned and skipped down the path singing, "The Wonderful Wizard of Oz."

Deedee tilted her head back and laughed. "He's great! He's a kid! And you're right . . . he is definitely fun . . . and he's definitely got his eyes on you!"

China stared after him. "Did we tell him we'd take breakfast to Magda?"

"Well, no. But we don't mind."

"It's not that. It's the way he said it."

Deedee put one hand on her hip. "What are you talking about?"

"Isn't it strange to you?"

"Really," Deedee said. "I have no clue what you're talking about."

China put her head down and turned to go up the path to the shack. "Never mind."

The wild, pounding beat and loud singing in Sweet Pea Lodge carried up to them. "I miss the singing," China said.

"We can go to the meetings you know," said Deedee.

"You don't really want to go, do you?"

"No. But you could."

China held up the thermos. "We have more important things to do right now."

The dog eagerly lapped up the concoction Rick had made for him. The girls decided since the dog was in such poor condition, they should ration out little bits every half hour.

As the night wore on, they noticed the dog seemed to gain strength. Sometime around 2 A.M., Deedee poked an orange Flintstone's children's vitamin down the dog's throat. Then they all fell asleep.

CHAPTER FOUR

A GIANT SLUG MOVED SLOWLY across the surreal world of fuschia-pink plants and kelly-green sky. Every inch the slug moved forward, he made a slurping, sucking sound. China lay in the middle of a pillowy soft lily pad, wondering when the slug would cease his movements so she could keep sleeping. The slurping-sucking stopped, and China felt herself smile and drift away.

The slug suddenly hit her in the face, clinging for a moment, then fell off. It hit her again, then fell off. Her hand brushed the empty air trying to make contact with the slug before it got her again. Contact!

Her mind struggled to make sense of the data as the slug now attacked her hand. It didn't have a hard shell at all. It was soft and furry.

"You silly thing!" a voice called out in China's dream. "Come over here and let China sleep. You're obviously feeling much better. Let's get you outside before you wet in here."

China rolled over and moaned. *Why would Deedee be talking to a slug? Slugs don't wet. They slime.* She scooched down in her sleeping bag, curling her hand underneath her cheek.

The dog! Her eyes popped open. No fuschia plants. No green sky. Only dust motes dancing in the sunlight that sliced through the wood slats. She flipped over. No dog. Sticking her head out the door, she called in a whisper. "Deedee!"

Deedee rounded the corner, a bony bundle in her arms. "He's better, China! He's much better."

The little dog wiggled out of Deedee's arms and walked cockeyed to China.

"Hey!" Deedee exclaimed, "he looks like you did after you did the Washing Machine."

"Funny," China said, chuckling.

"We're going to need a collar and chain or leash to make sure he doesn't run away or follow us while we're gone."

China put her tennis shoe on, tying the tie into a double bow. "I hate the idea of locking him up, but I guess it's better for him." She reached over and tousled the little guy's head. "Where do we get one?"

"There's a small general store up the road about two miles. They usually have one of everything. Dusty, dirty, hidden in the rafters . . . but they've got it."

The morning passed with end-to-end tasks. First, Magda's breakfast of one egg fried hard and white buttered toast had to be delivered. A very cheerful Rick had another pot of slop simmering for the girls when they returned with Magda's empty tray, and they took it to the maintenance shed. The little dog lapped up the cooling brew, thanking each of the girls with a hearty lick and a growing brightness in his eyes. Then they looked for Kemper, who put them to work while the teams played 100 mph dodgeball. Deedee fell right into place encouraging small clutches of shy girls to participate in the games. China preferred throwing padded catcher's gear and helmets over the players and ripping them off when they returned from the onslaught of tennis balls shot at them from launchers.

"It's a perfect excuse to put your hands on the cutest guys in camp," China explained to Deedee later, as they trudged up the street to the general store.

Deedee shook her head, her hair looking like Spanish tile in the sun. "I need to hang around you more, China. You help me to see the error of my ways."

The sun slowly added color to their skin without the girls being aware of it. The trees swayed and "chattered" in the breeze. Squirrels darted in and out, up and down trees, scolding if the girls got too close. Occasionally a car sped by, blowing crackly leaves and dirt into the air. They talked. They walked without talking. They skipped. They looked carefully around to be sure no one watched, then they linked arms and galloped in a lurching gait down the road singing "We're off to see the Wizard" at the top of their lungs, like Rick had done the night before.

China dropped her head back and laughed, pulling Deedee to a stop. "Hark! The road turneth away from thee and me!"

"Double hark!" Deedee responded, "there waveth a paper from yonder tree."

"Hi, paper!" China called, waving madly. "Come, dear, mustn't be rude, wave to the nice paper."

Deedee's arm moved in a proper queenly wave.

"Wait!" commanded China. "I think I doth see something horrendous and unthinkable!"

"What, pray tell, could that be?" Deedee said, shading her eyes with her hand, her head swiveling back and forth like a lighthouse beam searching the sea.

China put her hands on her hips, indignant. "Someone hath stapled that paper to a living tree. How darest they!"

"My word," Deedee proclaimed, scratching her scalp with one finger. "Whatever shall we do?"

"We shall rescue the tree, Sir Deeds!" She thrust her invisible sword forward, following its lead across the street and up the grade to the suffering tree.

Deedee marched behind, her boots clumping ferociously on the pavement.

China yanked the paper off the tree, crumpled it, and tossed it over her shoulder. Deedee caught it.

"There, there," cooed China to the tree, stroking the bark tenderly. "I'll take those awful staples out of your skin in no time. I'll do it quickly so it won't hurt."

China jammed her stubby thumbnail underneath the staple and wiggled it out.

"Oh, no!" wailed Deedee.

"That is not a knightly tone, my friend," China said without looking back. She started to loosen a second staple.

"We won't be needing any dog junk," Deedee said softly.

China whirled around. "What are you talking about?"

Deedee held the uncrumpled sheet of paper in her hands so China could read it.

LOST

Small, black, curly-haired

mutt. Part poodle.

JOEY

1405 Twisted Bow Lane

China plopped into the dirt. "Joey" was all she said.

Deedee sat next to her and hugged her knees. "It fits him."

China sighed. "I should have known." She picked up a hunk of pine needles that looked like a miniature broom and swept the dirt with them. "I should have known it was too good to be true. I've always wanted a dog. Someone I could talk to . . ."

"Thanks a lot. What am I? Stone soup?"

China gave her an ugly look. "You aren't a dog."

"Well, thank you very much. I've been worried

about that."

"It's just that you can cuddle a dog, you know? I can't sit around cuddling another person. As little kids we could cuddle stuffed animals. Now we have to hide if we're doing that. But I can hug a dog right out in the open. No one gives it a second thought. And a dog doesn't talk back when I need to blow off steam. A dog listens. And I never have to worry that a dog will tell my secrets."

"I wouldn't either," Deedee promised.

"I know . . . it's just different."

Deedee nodded her understanding. She picked up a pebble and tossed it. Her long fingers searched in the dirt for another. And another. She piled them up in her hand and tossed them, one by one.

"I should have known it was too good to believe that God would answer my prayer like that. Dogs just don't appear out of nowhere."

A 1965 blue Impala sped by, swirling dirt into their faces. The girls coughed, flailing the dust clouds with their arms and hands

"They're stopping," Deedee said, pointing to the brake lights. The white reverse lights came on, the car fishtailing backwards. The passenger door creaked a protest as it flew open.

"Can I join this pity party, or is it private?" Rick grinned his killer smile.

China cocked her head. "Private." She used her fingers to comb her hair away from her face.

"Need a ride back to camp?"

The girls looked at each other. "Thanks," Deedee said, wiping the dirt off the seat of her pants as she stood. She put out her hand for China, who grabbed it and pulled herself up.

Deedee pushed China in the car first, then climbed in behind her.

"So what's the sad news?" asked Rick.

Neither girl spoke. Both stared out the front window.

"Maybe I can help."

China bit her tongue, wondering if he really could. "Our little dog is lost."

"Where'd you lose him?"

"No," Deedee corrected. "Someone else lost him and is looking for him." She held the paper out so he could see it while he drove. Rick glanced at it, nodded, then flicked a lever to turn on the blinker. He slowed the car and moved onto Lakeview Road.

"Well, isn't that great? He has a home. Someone who loves him."

Deedee looked at China. "We love him."

China looked at her watch, then at Rick. "Aren't you supposed to be serving lunch in about 30 minutes?"

Rick nodded, pulling into Deedee's driveway. "I ran out of something. Had to run to the store to get it. I'll see you at 3:00, right?"

"Right," China said without enthusiasm.

The girls picked at their lunch in silence. Eve and

Adam talked enough to fill the void. Afterwards, the girls walked to the boat shack where Deedee needed to begin her afternoon work.

"When will we take the dog back?" China asked.

"Tomorrow morning would be a good time. I'll tell Kemper we won't be able to help him with the Mud Pit games."

China cringed. "I don't know if I could ever go back there again."

China left Deedee at the boat shack and made her way through the forest to the maintenance shed. She fed the dog bits of the sandwich she hadn't eaten. He gobbled the bologna and spit out the tomato.

After he finished, they sat across the shack from each other. "Joey!" she said, smiling. She patted the floor in front of her. He tried to trot, but could only walk cockeyed. He flopped in her lap and looked up at her. Her eyes filled with tears. "So it's true, then," she said to him. "You really do belong to someone else. Come on. Let's go out and do the basic body function routine."

She picked him up off her lap, depositing him on the floor. Pulling open the door, she walked out with a little black shadow at her heels. She rounded the corner of the shack into the sunshine and headed for a boulder where she could sit while the dog sniffed around and made himself happy.

As she reached the boulder, the dog started to bark viciously. China turned to look at him. His jaws snapped and she could see froth collecting in the corners of his mouth. "Joey?" she said, backing away from him toward the rock. *Rabies*, she thought. *How stupid we didn't think of rabies. These mountains must be full of it.*

She squatted to the ground, "It's okay, Joey. It's okay."

The dog snarled and snapped, moving closer to her and then around her, still snapping and snarling. For the first time, China realized he wasn't snarling at her. He moved his bony body between China and the rock. Then China heard the rattle. She could barely see the camouflaged snake in a hollow beside the boulder.

China inched backwards, trying to move slowly and not frighten the swaying head into striking. The barking continued until the dog sounded hoarse. Every inch China moved back, the dog moved with her, keeping himself between her and the snake.

It took little effort and not much time, but sweat dripped down China's back and she panted as though she had run the whole way up the hill. She moved around the shed into the shade, leaning her back against the slats, and slid down into a sitting position. Then she breathed.

The dog came up to her, licking her hand, his tail beating the air. "You want approval, don't you, you silly thing?" She scooped him up and nuzzled his neck, holding him close until the shaking stopped. "How can I give you up now?"

CHAPTER FIVE

RICK LOOKED UP FROM THE OPEN BIBLE in front of him and glanced at his watch as China walked in. "Good girl! Five minutes early. Okay, get your apron on and let's get to work."

China crossed the ties of the apron in the back, tying them in the front. "Okay, Boss," she said, trying to be cheerful. "What's first?"

Rick smiled, nodding his approval. "Good, good, she knows her rightful place." He closed his Bible and put it on a high shelf near the back door. "Every night we have salad bar so the skinny girls who are eternally on diets, or afraid to eat in front of boys, will have something to nibble on. We can't let the species die out, now, can we?"

I don't get Rick at all, China thought, watching every move he made. His eyes danced with pure delight. His smile moved across his face without any resistance at all. People would call it a genuine smile. *His words sound kind of rude, but every bone in his*

44

body says he's teasing. When did I get overly sensitive to people? Why does he have to be so ugly?

Rick pointed to the walk-in refrigerator. "We need four dozen eggs and 15 heads of iceberg lettuce and four each of the romaine and spinach. Would you be the kind and dutiful slave God created you to be and get them for us, please?" He did a little soft shoe and sang happy nonsense words to a light nonsense tune.

China followed him with her eyes, trying desperately to decide if she should punch his lights out or laugh. *Heather. That's when I got too sensitive.* The fight went out of China. *Because of Heather I guess now I don't trust as easily as I used to.* She moved to the walk-in and yanked on the silver handle. The heavy door swung open. She left it open, and walked into the chilly air looking for the eggs and lettuce. *It's not fair to judge Rick because of Heather or because of his looks. He's only trying to make me feel more comfortable by joking, that's all. Surely I can take a joke.*

China found the cartons of eggs and started to pile them in her arms. Never good at math, she took a moment to decide how many cartons of 18 eggs would make four dozen. "Dummy," she muttered to herself after standing there staring at the cartons. "Eighteen is a dozen and a half . . ." She grabbed three cartons and took them to the preparation table. Back into the cold, she moved a couple of blue, slatted plastic crates to get to the lettuce. The door swung shut, a loud click telling her it latched.

China couldn't move. Her old fears raced back to swirl around her mind and confuse her. Dark. Cold. In a box. She knew the fears were stupid. She was just a dumb seven-year-old kid who thought sleeping in a box in the backyard would be fun. But she woke terrified and never got over the fear of being in the dark, in the cold, in a closed place.

"Rick?" she called, her voice stopped by the insulated walls and double fans on each side of the refrigerator blowing cold air. Where the door should be, she saw a round, green glow. She ran to it and pounded with the palm of her hand. The door easily popped open and she ran out, breathing fast and heavy.

Rick leaned against the prep table, his arms crossed, a Dodger's cap perched off-center on his blond curls. "Never," he said calmly, "leave the door open. It costs a lot of money to run that refrigerator, and I won't have the honchos seeing the utility bill going sky high the week I ran the kitchen. It just won't do." His voice was gentle but firm. Kind of like China's dad when she had done something to be corrected for.

China shuddered.

"Why you're scared, aren't you?"

China nodded.

Rick tilted his head. "You know, you are even cuter when you're scared."

"I'm sorry I left the door open. I . . . I've always been afraid of being in a small place in the dark and the cold."

Rick shook his head. "It's not that small in there. The light switch is out here." He pointed to a switch with a red light indicator on the steel casing around the door. "When the red light is on, the light is on inside the walk-in. Even if the light is accidentally shut off, you still have the glowing handle to guide you. You'll get used to it," he said kindly. "Now get the lettuce. Time's wasting."

China flipped the light switch and went inside, closing the door behind her. "It's a small room, see?" she told her scared little-girl self. "It's not a box and it's not dark. It's a room."

It took two trips to bring out the lettuce. She lined it all up on the prep table.

"Chop up all the lettuce into bite-size pieces," Rick instructed, "and boil the eggs until hard. Can you do that?"

"Sure."

China found the pots where she had remembered they were kept from her KP duty the week before. She filled a big one with water and put it on the great gas stove, turning the burner on high underneath it.

While waiting for it to boil, she started to wash the spinach and romaine lettuces by hand, letting the leaves dry on clean white towels.

When the water boiled, she added the raw eggs, one by one, lowering them into the water with a slotted spoon. Her movements were slow and careful, every motion a result of high concentration.

"What are you doing?" came a laughing voice beside her.

The voice startled her, and an egg slipped from the slotted spoon and crashed on the floor. She looked up into John's amused face.

"I'm boiling the eggs like Rick told me to."

"Maybe that's what you think you're doing." John wagged his head. "I thought everyone knew how to boil eggs."

"I do . . ." China started to protest.

"I thought it was common sense. Look. You put the eggs in first. Then add some cold water and put the fire on low to medium. It helps the eggs to adjust to the heat slowly. When you add cold eggs to hot water . . . look." John pointed into the bubbling water. White filaments of cooked egg drifted away from the cracked shells like escaping worms.

"Oh," said China, feeling incredibly stupid.

"No problem," John said cheerfully. He tapped the side of her head. "Next time, use what God gave you up here or ask Rick or me. We know how to do it all."

Why do I feel so stupid? China forced a thin smile.

She set the timer and turned to work on the lettuce. With a small knife she dug around the iceberg lettuce heart. It came out looking like a whitish stop sign. She waved at John and held it up like a trophy.

John looked over his shoulder. "Rick! Where are you? Your prize worker needs more help."

"What?" came a voice from the back, "I've got my hands full."

John shook his head. "Another lesson in the kitchen of life," he said, picking up a head of lettuce. "Rick neglected to consider that not everyone has the capability to know simple kitchen tasks." He whacked the head of lettuce, heart side down, on the side of the table. He touched the heart, and like magic it came out intact, leaving only the lettuce behind.

Rick came around the corner, a stack of pans in his arms. "John! We've got to get that cake mixed and in the oven pronto!"

China blinked quickly, hoping they didn't see the tears welling up in her eyes. She picked up a head of lettuce and slammed it on the counter.

China's only break came hours later—a brief 10 minutes to take Magda her dinner. Deedee came along.

Magda lay on her side and didn't say or do much. "I really think I should tell Daddy," Deedee said.

"It's okay," Magda said weakly. "I feel fine for awhile. And then suddenly I get this piercing headache and strange body spasms that last for about an hour. Then it goes away again. I'm sure I'll be fine in a day or so."

"I sure hope so," China said emphatically. "I miss you in the kitchen."

"Rick's a good worker, China. I'm sure he's doing fine in the kitchen."

"He is, Magda. Everything is running smoothly." China sighed. "But I do have a lot to learn."

"A little learning never hurt anyone. Rick came to see me. He thinks you're great. I think he kind of has a crush on you," Magda admitted.

"You do?" China's stomach did a funny flip.

"Of course he does," Deedee chimed in. "He watches everything you do."

"But I don't want him to like me," China protested.

"Why not?" Magda asked.

"His looks bother me. Especially that look behind his eyes," China said.

Both Magda and Deedee stared at her like she had lost her mind.

"Forget it," China said, faking a smile. *I'm crazy. I'm being judgmental like Heather. I'm reacting as if he's a Heather, and Rick is certainly not Heather.*

"Now you be nice to him," Magda said, wagging her finger weakly. "He might be 24, but he's been through an awful lot and sometimes acts like a little boy."

"Don't worry," China said, hoping she could make good on her promise.

After a quick glance at the clock on the wall, China knew she had to get back to work. Deedee left with her to tend the dog.

Outside the kitchen, China gave Deedee a stack of bologna and a couple of old biscuits, telling her to be extra nice to him.

"He saved me from a rattlesnake today."

Deedee's eyes grew wide. "He did?"

China nodded. "It was on the boulder outside the shack. Be careful, okay?"

"I will. And I'll give the sweetie an extra hug." Deedee turned to leave, and China opened the screen door. "I can't call him Joey, can you?" Deedee asked.

"I tried. But it didn't feel right. I'm going to cry tomorrow."

"That's okay. So will I."

China moved into the kitchen, putting Magda's lunch tray with the dinner dishes that were fast being delivered to the kitchen by the KP helpers. Rick assigned her to the back room to rinse the dishes and put them through the high-powered washer. As she sprayed the garbage off the dishes, tears poured down her face. She jumped when she felt two hands hold her shoulders. "What's wrong?" the gentle voice asked her.

She dared not turn around. She knew she would be 12 inches closer to that face she couldn't look at without her whole insides trying to back away. And she might not be able to be careful as she promised Magda. Her shoulders started to shake with the combination of sobs for the dog and trembling at the touch of someone so close.

"What's wrong?" Rick repeated, letting go of her shoulders.

"I don't want him to go back home," China explained.

"Him?" Rick asked, backing off a couple of steps.

China turned to face him. "The dog."

Rick's tender expression became stern. "I don't understand, China. You're crying over a dog that doesn't even belong to you? Tears are a waste of time. They never bring anything you love back to you."

China wiped her tears.

"Be strong. Be glad the dog has a home. Let go of what doesn't belong to you." Rick brushed away a few strands of her hair that had escaped the rubber band. "Aren't tears a weakness? As Christians, we should be strong in the Lord. If it doesn't have eternal value, let it go."

China sighed. "You're right." She sighed again, to help make the tears stop. "Thanks."

"Anytime."

Rick left, and for the rest of the evening, China held back her tears, knowing they were only selfish and God did not want her to be selfish, but giving. *God, why do you always ask us to do things that are so hard?*

The hardest part would be tomorrow morning. And she didn't want to face that. Not now. Not ever.

CHAPTER SIX

"**C**AN I CARRY HIM FIRST?" China asked Deedee the following morning.

"Yeah."

Once in the open, the dog was like a magnet. Practically every kid in camp wanted to touch him.

"Oh, how cute!" Cooed a girl with "Angela" scripted across the front of her sleeveless sweatshirt.

"What's his name?" asked the heavy girl with Angela.

"Cool. A dog," commented a lanky kid with his shorts dangling loosely from his waist, his blond hair long and free.

"You gonna let him go to the Mud Pit with us?" called a jock as he ran by.

The girls shivered.

"He's a bag of bones. Don't you ever feed him?"

"Poor baby. He's been lost, I bet."

"You sweet thing."

"Oh, bring him to the beach today so we can play."

53

The girls didn't answer. Soon they left the sea of kids and made it to the road. Deedee took over carrying him. "We could let him walk some."

"Yeah, but let's save his strength." China petted his head.

Tears dribbled down Deedee's face. She looked at China's dry cheeks. "How come you're not crying?"

China sighed and clenched her teeth to hold back the tears. "Rick reminded me last night that it's selfish to cry when it isn't even my dog. I should be happy the dog has a loving family waiting for him."

Deedee's tears came even faster. "So why is it wrong to cry if something hurts you? Even if the tears don't make any sense, I think it's okay to cry."

"Maybe God doesn't want us to cry. It's a weakness, isn't it?"

Deedee stopped, flinging her deep red curls out of her face. She shifted the dog and looked at China, opened her mouth a couple of times, then closed it for good and started walking up the hill again.

China continued to look at Deedee, hoping for an answer. "As Christians we're to be strong in the Lord."

Deedee shook her head slowly. "The words are from the Bible, that's for sure. But I don't think . . . I don't know. Jesus cried when His friend died."

They walked in silence for another few minutes. "Up this way," Deedee said, gesturing toward a street with her head.

Neither said another word until they arrived at the

house on Twisted Bow.

"You're home," China whispered to the bundle of fur as Deedee handed him over.

A woman dressed in a tie-dyed ankle-length skirt answered Deedee's knock.

"We found your dog," China said, scratching the dog's ear.

The woman looked surprised and turned to call behind her. "Fred . . . come here."

A scruffy-looking mountain man thumped through the house to the door. "What's the problem, Carla?"

He looked at the girls and the bundle in China's arms. "Your dog," Deedee offered.

"It sure looks like him, doesn't it, Fred?" moaned the woman.

"If he had some meat on his bones they could almost be twins."

China shifted her weight and asked, "How can you be sure he's not yours?"

The woman bit her lip, her eyes filling with tears.

"Our Joey was hit by a car. We found him as we drove home from the store one day. I don't know who this one belongs to."

China's heart skipped a beat.

"But we'd love to take him and help him get better," the woman suggested, wiping her eyes.

China and Deedee looked at each other. "We need to talk a second," Deedee told them. She turned China around by the arm. "It would be the best thing for him."

"I know," China whispered. "But I can't say good-bye."

"My dad will never let us keep him. And we can't keep him hidden forever. These people will take him. Maybe we should leave him."

China turned around and handed the woman the dog. He looked at China, his eyes filled with confusion and hurt. "It's okay," she told him. "You'll have a good home here."

Deedee petted him one last time, her tears traveling silently down her cheeks. She kissed him and walked away.

Fred moved to close the door. "Wait!" China said. "Will you take our phone number? Just in case?"

Carla had already disappeared into the house. Fred nodded and also disappeared, reappearing a moment later with a napkin and a felt-tip pen.

China scribbled Deedee's name and phone number on it, then shoved it back at Fred who looked at it and said, "Thanks, Deedee."

China didn't bother to correct him. This time she couldn't stop the tears. *Dear God, I guess I'm totally weak.*

The girls reached Deedee's house in time for another silent lunch. Afterwards, they walked to the boat shack. China stared at her shoes the whole way. Images of a small black dog moved across the screen of her mind.

"What're you going to do?" Deedee asked when

they reached the boat shack. "Are you going to stay here with me?"

China shrugged her shoulders. "I think I'd bring you down too much."

"I'm already at the bottom."

China shook her head. "Maybe I'll go up to the prayer chapel and tell God what I think."

"Whoa!" Deedee said, taking the key out of the cash box to unlock and unchain the boats. "I'll keep my eye out for a bolt of lightning. Should I tell anyone that I know why the prayer chapel suddenly burned down?"

China barely smiled. "You're a toad, Deedee Kiersey. A genuine toad."

Deedee hugged her. "And you're a frog, China Jasmine Tate."

China helped Deedee remove the chains from the boats, then walked around the lake to the prayer chapel. It took more strength than she imagined to open the heavy oak door. Inside, she slipped off her shoes, the flattened stones cool beneath her bare feet. *Holy,* she whispered. She looked at the 13 stained-glass windows. Six on each side of the chapel. The 12 disciples surrounded her. At the front of the small chapel, the thirteenth window. Jesus kneeling in the garden, praying his heart out. *God wouldn't strike me dead for saying how I feel. Jesus did.* She clapped her hand over her mouth. *Yeah, and Jesus died a horrible death a few hours later.*

She almost backed out of the chapel, but another thought brought her back. *Well, God knows how I feel anyway, so I guess I would be lying if I didn't tell Him or pretended I wasn't upset.*

She walked reverently to the front of the chapel and knelt on a red vinyl cushion, resting her hands on the wooden railing. She looked up at the broken pieces of glass remarkably put together to make the beautiful picture.

"Hi, Jesus. Guess we both want God's attention." She sighed and rocked back onto her heels. "God?" She licked her lips. "I just thought I'd tell you I'm kinda mad that we don't get to keep that little dog. I don't know. I feel like he's real special. Like he and I are buddies." She thought a minute. "He did save me, you know."

Tears started to well up and drip down her cheeks. "I wish sometimes that you wouldn't take away everything that's special to me. Remember when I was little and my parents decided to be missionaries? That meant they went through all my toys and only let me keep five things. And I didn't even get to choose. I wish you still wouldn't take things away from me."

China rested her forehead on the railing. In the silence came a realization. *God let me stay here this summer. He let me keep Deedee. She's the first person who has ever accepted me just as I am. The only person I've ever really enjoyed being around.*

"Uhh, thanks, God, for letting me keep Deedee . . .

at least for the summer." Her heart hurt again, remembering that after the summer it was back to Guatemala and beans and Spanish and all the MK kids who were nice . . . but she just didn't click with.

"Oh. And I guess I'd like you to help me see Rick as a buried treasure instead of always seeing the stuff on the outside that makes me queasy.

"Thanks for listening, God. I don't guess I'll ever understand you, but I'm glad you say you understand me."

China walked to the door and slipped on her shoes. She blinked at the bright sunshine and without thinking, she moved through the trees and walked up the steps to Eelapuash, the great dining hall. The Indian name, *Eelapuash*, meaning "sore belly," always made her laugh inside. Once inside the kitchen, Rick smiled at her. "Ahh! She's come to see us early! My beautiful girl! My great, wonderful worker is even greater!"

Some of China's sadness melted away. Maybe God was bringing all kinds of people who cared about her into her life, and a little dog really wasn't that important.

The afternoon passed quickly. China cooked pounds of hamburger until crumbly, then Rick took over to work magic and make it delicious chili. She chopped zillions of tomatoes and onions. Grated pounds and pounds of cheese. She danced the polka around the kitchen with Rick and John, while Carolyn clapped her hands and whooped and hollered. They laughed and told bad elephant and knock-knock jokes until they were outrageously silly. They watched the high school kids go through the buffet line piling gobs of stuff on their baked potatoes. Within minutes, all China's hard work had disappeared into gaping, gobbling mouths.

She divided her own potato into quarters and put chili and cheese on one, tomatoes and onions on another, broccoli and cheese on a third, and a glop of butter on the fourth. Between mouthfuls, she told funny stories about practical jokes she and other missionary families had played in Guatemala.

In the middle of the chaos, the screen door flew open, and Deedee marched in. "China!" she bellowed. "We have to talk. Right now!" She grabbed China's arm that had been in the process of moving a chili n' cheese bite to her mouth, removed the fork, and put it on the plate. "We'll be right back," she announced to the rest of the crew.

"But . . ." China protested, "I'm in the middle of . . ."

"Just come with me. You can finish later."

Deedee dragged China out the door. "I got home for dinner, and guess what?"

"What?" China asked impatiently.

"There was a message for me on the phone."

"And? So?" China pulled the scrunchie from her hair, combed her hair back with her fingers, and put the scrunchie back in.

"From those people. The mountain hippies."

China's brown eyes grew wide. "Yeah?"

"I called them back. They don't want the dog. They're going to take him to the pound if we don't come get him tomorrow."

China's eyes grew dark. "Why? What's wrong?"

Deedee stopped dancing around. "Well, that's the funny part. They won't tell me. They said just to come get him. She sounded mad."

"Mad?"

"Maybe he's not housebroken or something."

"Or maybe he has worms and we didn't notice."

"So?" Deedee said. "Are we going to go get him?"

"Of course. Without a doubt."

"But that's another day of not helping Kemper."

China thought. "Isn't tomorrow the day the families come to the lake?"

"Oh, yeah. Then I don't have to go to work until 2:30. We'll have time to do both."

They high-fived and went back into the kitchen. Three anxious faces stared at them, waiting for the information. "It's nothing," China said, grinning from ear to ear.

"You lie," Rick said, smiling back. "Tell us."

"My dad then snuck around the back of the house," China said, continuing her story where she had left off.

"Not that!" Rick protested. "What's the deal?"

"I have to take Magda her dinner now," Deedee announced, taking the prepared tray and heading for the door. "See you in a bit."

"Come on, now, that's not fair," John said.

"Tell us or else," Rick threatened with a glob of butter poised in his spoon.

"You wouldn't dare," China said.

The words were still hanging in the air when the butter landed on her forehead. "You creep!" China laughed, scooping a bite from her plate and whipping it back. Rick leaned to one side and it landed beyond him in a bin of clean silverware.

"OOOOH!" chorused John and Carolyn.

Rick casually looked over his shoulder. "I guess someone has a mess to clean up."

China popped a bite of tomatoes and onions into her mouth, the butter from her face now buried in a napkin. "I wonder who that could be."

Rick stood, walked over to China and said, "I think I'll assign you to clean up the mess." As he walked by, he pretended to trip. "Oops!" The contents of his plate slid into her lap. "Oh, I'm so sorry!" he said in a totally fake voice.

China gasped. John and Carolyn burst into laughter.

"Dinner's over!" Rick announced as he peered into the dining hall.

China cleaned up the mess, her mind thinking, plotting, waiting for the right moment. It didn't come until after Deedee had returned with Magda's tray, telling China nothing had changed.

After Deedee left, China stood in the dishwashing

pit, spraying plates with the mighty hose sprayer. She heard Rick approach. She pretended she didn't hear him, then spun around, sprayer in hand, nailing him with a full blast of cold water to the chest. For a final touch, she swept the hose up to his face. She did it so fast, he didn't have time to flinch. She smiled. "Bull's-eye."

She turned around and continued to spray the dishes as though nothing had happened.

A few minutes later a cold ooze began at the top of her head and glopped from her hair to her back, over her face to her shoulders and chest. The ooze smelled of peaches. As it froze her nose and dripped off the end, she turned slowly to face the only person who could have done such a thing. "You're so cute," she told Rick.

"I know. I work at it." He blew her a kiss, then walked out.

China leaned toward the hole in the wall where the dirty dishes were shoved through from the kitchen. "What am I supposed to do? Can I go change?"

Rick's face appeared in the hole. "No," he said sweetly. "Yogurt won't hurt you any. Finish up."

China didn't know whether to laugh or scream. The yogurt wasn't quite so cold any more, but it still felt totally gross as it found its way under her shirt and into her ears. She pushed the dishes aside, stuck her head over the sink, and hosed herself off.

Her heart was beating in a funny way. She shivered,

not from the cold, but from something else. *Stop it!*
she told herself. *What's wrong with you, anyway?*
You're getting on my nerves.

CHAPTER SEVEN

WHEN THE DISHES WERE ALL WASHED, dried, and put away, China stepped outside the kitchen where Deedee waited for her. But the darkness hid China's condition, and it wasn't until they passed under a light that Deedee stopped and asked, "What happened to you?"

"Food fight."

"Whew! If you didn't lose, I'd hate to see the loser."

China forced a smile. "I want to get cleaned up. This stuff feels gross."

They walked briskly past the lake, across the battlefield, and into the woods. "What do you want to do after you clean up?"

"You're going to think I'm crazy."

"I always think you're crazy," Deedee said affectionately.

"Thank you."

"You're welcome."

"I miss going to the evening meetings."

Deedee didn't respond.

"I know you hate it," China added.

"I don't hate it." Deedee freed her hair from the alligator clip, shaking it gently to let the curls fly free. "I just overloaded on meetings."

"Would you hate it if we went?"

"Actually . . . no."

Later, inside Sweet Pea Lodge, China and Deedee chose seats close to the front, but off to one side. China looked around the room at the new additions to the atmosphere. Pasted all over the walls of the lodge were large cardboard insects. Black Widows throwing cardboard water balloons at swarms of angry Locusts. Scorpions guarding a mud pit, while Stink Bugs and Tarantulas raced each other carrying old, iron beds.

The kids seemed to have gotten used to each other after the awkwardness of Sunday. They sang at the top of their lungs with the amplified guitars blasting music into the room. They draped their arms around each other's shoulders and swayed. They clapped and stomped and did wild hand motions to "Pharaoh, Pharaoh." China and Deedee joined right in. The kids recognized them as the helpers and welcomed them as friends.

Kemper opened with bizarre stories he'd gathered from tabloids. A baby born with angel wings. Horses born with human heads. A lady whose lips accidentally got suctioned away during plastic surgery.

Another who died on her balcony overlooking a busy street, and sat there for two weeks before anyone noticed. He moved into talking about loving and caring for those around us. The same message as the previous week. But different. New examples. Same concepts. The words filtered through ears that were different. Ears that had lived through Heather for a whole week and survived.

"Pretend these tabloid stories were true," Kemper said. "Would you accept these people as friends? Or would you reject them because they look and act differently than what you consider normal?"

China's heart accused her. *You're not accepting Rick because he doesn't look perfect. Is that fair?*

"Remember, Kemper's little sister died," Deedee whispered behind her hand, bringing China back to the meeting.

China nodded. *She was sick. And different. People made fun of her funny looks and the stuff she did. But Kemper loved her.*

China eagerly listened to Kemper as his words took on deeper meaning. New meaning. They were from someone who knew. Who understood pain . . . understood weakness. A guy who cared about more than "male bonding." She tried to open her mind wider to understand and accept God's words about loving those not like herself, or those who didn't fit into her view of normal.

After the meeting, the girls walked slowly back to

Deedee's house, where they undressed and crawled into bed.

"Deedee," China hissed from her sleeping bag bed on the floor. "I can't sleep."

"Me neither." Deedee rolled over, hanging her head off the bed to talk to China. "Tomorrow we get our baby back."

The next day during the competition, both girls got bombarded with water balloons because their minds were on their dog and not their job. "At least the balloons didn't have purple food coloring in them," China said.

The walk to the cabin on Twisted Bow Lane didn't seem long or hot. But the stone steps to the front door seemed higher than before. The girls took them two at a time, Deedee not winded at all, China not paying any attention to her own breath that came in huffs. The girls linked pinkies for good luck, then Deedee knocked on the door. China's heart thumped hard in her chest. Some of her fast breathing had nothing to do with the long walk to the house.

Fred opened the door, Carla at his side with the dog in her arms. When he saw the girls, he started wagging his tail, which in turn, wagged his whole body against Carla's tie-dyed cotton blouse. Fred pushed open the screen door, and Carla shoved the dog into China's arms. "Here," she said gruffly.

China looked at her, confused. "Did he bite you?" she asked, thinking that could be the only reason for their attitude.

Deedee smiled. "We don't understand why you'd want to get rid of this precious pup."

Carla pulled the screen closed and locked it. "You should have told us."

The girls looked at each other, confusion mirrored in both their faces. "Told you what?" China asked.

Fred crossed his arms as if to challenge the girls' statement.

Carla sighed in disgust. "Don't tell me you didn't know. I simply can't believe you wouldn't know."

Fred looked intently at the girls, then touched his wife's arm. "Maybe they didn't have a chance to see it."

"See what?" Deedee said tossing her head like an impatient stallion. She crossed her arms and rocked back on her heels.

"The dog is deaf," Carla snapped. "And I don't believe you didn't know."

China's heart stopped. She could have sworn it did. All the blood from her body seemed to fall somewhere down around her ankles.

Deedee's pale face rivaled the white face of the moon. She turned to look at the dog and China, then back to the folks sheltered behind their screen door. "We didn't . . ."

"SO?" China said. "So what if he's deaf? Does that make him any less of a creature?" Words from Kemper's talk the night before flooded her mind.

Fred smiled as an adult sometimes does to a kid who, as far as he is concerned, is speaking totally irrational, immature nonsense. "I know you kids are idealistic. But there's a truth about this world you are too young to understand."

Deedee had her hands on her hips. "And what, pray tell, is that?"

"The world is getting too crowded. There are thousands of hungry people. And there is simply no room for a creature that has imperfections."

"What?" China shrieked, pulling the dog closer to her chest. "Are you telling us this sweet little guy has no reason to live because he's not perfect?"

Carla shifted, forcing her face to soften. "Look, don't you think it might be much kinder to put the dog out of its suffering?"

"He's not suffering," China insisted. "Except when he's around imbeciles like you!" She turned around and stomped down the stairs.

Deedee gave a quick, assenting nod and followed her.

The door to the house closed hard behind them. Not with a slam, but with the solid finality of someone sure of their opinion.

"Stupid people," China muttered.

"Do you really think he's deaf?" Deedee asked.

"I don't care if he is," snapped China.

"Put him down."

China put him down and tried to walk away. He

toddled after her, still leaning to one side. "Sit." The dog wagged his tail and panted happily, sitting at her feet.

"He understood that," China said. "He's not deaf."

"We don't know that he understood that. You stopped walking, and so did he."

"Fine. You try it."

"Come here!" Deedee called from behind him, her hair flying out as she jumped down to a squat. The dog spun on his heels and ran to her.

"Why did they think he was deaf?"

Deedee looked the dog in the face, holding his jaws in her hands. "I don't know, but maybe they just didn't like him."

"Come on, babe," China said, whistling softly. "Come back to Mama!"

"Mama!" Deedee exclaimed. "Whoever said you were his mama?" The dog's face, still in Deedee's hands, did not even try to turn around.

"Come here!" China called. Nothing happened. She waved her arms. "Yoohoo!" The dog pulled his head from Deedee's gentle grasp and turned around. China clapped her hands, and the dog went to her.

"Something's not right," China said, scratching his ears.

"He came when we both called," Deedee protested.

"Yeah, but he didn't budge until I waved my arms. You try. Sit real still but call him."

Deedee whistled, but the dog didn't move. She

shouted. She turned her back and clapped really hard.

"He's not even flinching," China said, her voice getting small.

"Go sit on the other side of that boulder," Deedee encouraged.

China picked up the dog and crouched on the ground where he couldn't see Deedee. She put him on the ground, where he had the freedom to move wherever he wanted.

On the other side of the rock, Deedee snapped, barked, yowled, called, clapped, and whistled her through-the-thumb-and-forefinger, ear-piercing whistle.

China plugged her ears. The dog sat, his black tail sweeping the dirt behind him, almost grinning at her. When Deedee appeared around the rock, he eagerly toddled to her.

Deedee sank into the dirt in front of China. "He's deaf," she admitted.

China sifted the dirt through her hands. "When he was barking at the rattlesnake, I called and called him, but he didn't even act as though he heard me. I just thought he had gone whacko on me."

In silence, they watched the dog flop happily in the dirt. He looked from one to the other, then crawled into China's lap. Deedee wiggled her fingers in front of her own crossed legs, and the dog went to her lap.

A small smile moved onto China's face. "Watch," she whispered to Deedee.

"Why're you whispering? He can't hear you anyway."

"Just watch." China wiggled her fingers, and the dog came to her.

Deedee smiled. "He may be deaf, but he's not stupid."

"We can teach him to obey sign language," China said.

Deedee thought. "We don't know sign language."

China stared at her. "So, we make up our own. Just so long as he knows what it is."

Deedee threw a pebble at China, her laughter suddenly erupting. "I was joking; can't you tell?"

"Course, silly." Inside, China wondered, *Maybe I can't tell anymore.*

The girls walked up to the general store and bought a royal blue collar and matching leash, a box of Snausage Dog Treats, and had just enough left over to buy Reeses Peanut Butter Cups for Deedee and Skittles for China.

The girls munched their candy and fed the dog treats whenever he sat at their sign of two fingers making an X. "We can't keep him in the shed anymore. He'd probably whine to get out," Deedee said.

"Do you think Magda would keep him?" China asked.

"Magda likes rules too much."

"Magda doesn't like rules."

"She honors them," Deedee insisted.

When their treats were gone, one girl carried the dog while the other carried the leash and the Snausage box. Every so often, they traded.

"Can't you talk to your dad?"

"I told you, he's allergic."

"Your mom?"

"I don't know."

China stopped in the middle of the street. "Rick!"

"Why Rick?"

"He gave us food for him and didn't tell. He said he had a dog when he was little. He even looked like he was crying about his dog."

"Crying? A male species crying? I think I like this person better all the time," Deedee said.

China opened her mouth to tell her not to like him too much, but then she closed her mouth again. *Better keep my problems to myself.*

"Want to ask him?" Deedee encouraged.

"It couldn't hurt."

Deedee smiled. "The way he likes you, I'm sure he'd do anything for you."

"Do you really think he likes me?" China tried not to choke on the words.

"Oh, come on. The dog's deaf . . . but are you blind?"

"It's just that, well . . ." China put the box under one arm and pulled her hair off her face.

"I'm listening."

China thought fast. She couldn't tell her it had to do with his looks. That she didn't want Rick to like her. Not even as a friend. It would be too embarrassing. "He says something nice while he's doing something mean."

"Mean? Like what?"

China thought.

"Go on," Deedee said. "I'm waiting."

"Like when he gave me the dog food. He held my wrists too tight and said I owed him. Don't you think someone who does something that makes you feel uncomfortable is doing it on purpose?"

"Not unless they're a jerk. Most people don't mean to do things like that."

"Remember the yogurt last night? Don't you think that was mean?"

Deedee laughed. "Time to switch loads. My arms are aching." They stopped and made the change. "If you hadn't retaliated with chili one time and water another, I'd say, yeah, that was a little extreme. But China, you asked for it. Don't you know the rule of food fights? Never get involved unless you're willing to get creamed . . ." she started laughing. "Literally."

China sighed. "You're right, I know you're right. And if it had been you and me in the exact same situation, with the exact same things happening, and you dumped a quart of peach yogurt on me, I would have laughed until I cried, then given you the biggest bear hug and rubbed my head all over you."

"So why is it different with Rick?"

"I don't know." China frowned, thinking hard.

Deedee probed gently. "Is it because you like him, too?"

Something popped inside China. "Are you kidding?" Her face flushed with shame.

"You told me you've never really had a boyfriend."

"Hah!" China laughed. "Not a chance in Guatemala. No one of cuteness or consequence."

"It could be that it scares you to have someone like you. You can't grab him, give him a bear hug, and smear him all over with yogurt."

China nodded. "That's too close. It's saying too much." *It's saying I like him when he grosses me out.*

"The first time I had a boyfriend I was terrified to talk to him, terrified I might say or do something really stupid, and terrified when he talked to me. Everything became wildly focused and out of focus at the same time."

"Are you better with guys now?"

Deedee laughed. "Only if they don't like me as anything more than a friend. I do great with males as long as I don't find them someone I'd like to get close to. The minute I think I'd like to be a special person in their life, I get weird again."

"I thought you were always weird."

Deedee smacked China over the head with the Snausage box.

"Ouch! You are a toad, Deedee."

"And you will always be a frog."

"Gee, thanks. I'm honored. Flattered. Pleased."

"Didn't you read the *Frog and Toad* books when you were a kid?"

"No," China admitted. "We didn't have many books when I was a kid. They were too costly to buy and ship to Guatemala."

Deedee smacked her forehead. "How stupid of me! Okay. Frog and Toad are best friends. They fight. They do fun things together. They're weird and wacky in their own ways. But they are always, always best friends. And they accept each other with all their warts and stupidities without condemning each other."

"Then, I accept your compliment with honor, Toad."

"Now that we have our names," Deedee smiled, "what do we call this little guy? Joey?"

"Naw. Bad luck to name anything living after something dead," China replied.

"Sammy?" said Deedee.

"Are you joking? I vote we wait awhile until he says or does something that gives us a clue about his personality."

"Says something?" Deedee asked.

"Sure."

"How do dogs say anything?"

China shrugged. "I don't know. But they do. Just like he said he was happy to see us when we got to the door of those awful people's house."

"He did say that, didn't he?"

"Of course. Now give the poor guy a chance to let us know what his name is."

"Yes, Sir China, oh mighty ruler."

"Deedee?"

"Yes?"

"Shut up."

CHAPTER EIGHT

THE THOUGHT OF ASKING RICK if he'd help them hide the dog made China's insides act up with a crazy ferocity. One part of her wanted the dog all to herself. She needed someone to love her no matter what stupid things she did. She didn't want to admit to another living soul the awful things that lived inside of her. But she could admit them to a dog, and he would still love her. She was fiercely jealous of that love and didn't want to share it with anyone.

The other side of her knew they needed help from someone who understood what loving a dog could be like. Someone who was willing to bend the rules for something good.

But she wasn't certain she knew Rick well enough to trust him. Should she play up to him and flirt with him? Some girls did that and got whatever they wanted. China kicked a rock. That wasn't her. Honesty flowed through her to a fault. She hated playing games with people. Hated bending and twisting things to her advantage. So she'd be straightforward with Rick. If he said no, he said no. It never hurts to ask, her father always told her. They can only say no.

"You're awfully quiet," Deedee said, tapping her arm.

China nodded, keeping her mouth shut.

The girls put the dog down on the ground, snapping the leash to his collar. "We'd better walk by the trail," Deedee suggested.

At the kitchen, China opened the screen door quietly and eased herself inside. She listened to the kitchen sounds, trying to catch the mood of the place before she approached Rick.

A silly song from Music Man, "Pick a Little, Talk a Little," came from the belly of the kitchen. The guys sang "Good-night, Ladies," in their best bass voices, while a lone female answered in her best cackle. China smiled. Perfect. She walked into their midst, stood next to Carolyn, and joined in. When the song ended, Rick bowed to China. "And to what do we owe this great honor?"

"I need to talk to you alone."

Rick's eyebrows raised. "Well!"

John winked at Rick.

China rolled her eyes. "Oh, brother. You guys are nuts." She turned and walked out of the kitchen, letting the screen door slam behind her.

Moments later, the door slammed again. "What's the big secret? You finally asking me out?"

China blushed. "Cute," she said, trying to hide her embarrassment.

Deedee appeared from around the back corner of the building, the little dog trotting beside her, leaning at a crazy angle.

"Oh," Rick cooed, his voice suddenly soft and mushy. A mother's voice seeing her baby for the first time. "He's so . . ." Rick tilted his head, as if looking at the dog with a tilt would make the dog straight. ". . . drunk."

"He's not drunk," China snorted.

"He's deaf," Deedee said. "We think he walks at an angle because his equilibrium is off or something."

Rick gathered him up in his huge arms. "He's adorable. Skinny, but adorable." He buried his face in the black, curly fur and moved it about, snuffling softly.

"What's his name?" he asked, lifting his head.

"We haven't decided yet," said China.

Rick moved his fingers through the fur. "I think he's part poodle."

"That's what we thought," agreed Deedee.

"We were hoping you could help us," China said cautiously.

"How?"

"We need a place for him to stay at night, and sometimes during the day. He's healthy enough to where he won't stay in the shack without yelping."

"Why don't you take him home?"

"Dad would never let me have a dog," Deedee said. "We've tried before, but he always said no."

Rick nodded, playing with the dog's fur. The dog turned to look at him, then gave his hand a swipe with his tongue. "I think he probably doesn't shed since he's part poodle. So we could have him in the kitchen without getting hair into everything."

China glanced quickly at Deedee, then bit her lip, trying not to hope too much.

"I know I could keep him in my cabin at night. That's no problem at all," Rick said.

"But he's still my dog," China reminded him.

"Our dog," Deedee added softly.

"He's still yours. But if he behaves, he can hang around here as much as necessary. But how will we hide him when someone shows up? What about when Magda comes back?"

China chewed on the inside of her cheek. "We're thinking hard on this. We hope we can have an answer in a couple of days or so."

Rick nodded. He opened the screen door. "Let's introduce him to the others."

The little guy walked in with a tilt that made them all laugh. Rounding corners, it looked as though he just might run into something. His brown eyes widened with determination, the whites showing. His tail wagged furiously when he made it without running into the corner of something. It was his own applause.

Over and over, China tried teaching him to sit when she hit two fingers from one hand onto the two fingers of the other. Deedee pushed his tail end to the ground as soon as China made the motion. Then they both clapped their hands, smiled, patted his head, and rewarded him with a Snausage. After awhile, he seemed uninterested in Snausages, so they left him to roam the kitchen.

"The health department would have a fit," Rick muttered. "Mr. Kiersey would have my hide," he said, and stared at Deedee. "If you weren't in on this I wouldn't even consider it. I'm banking on the idea that your dad would have leniency knowing his precious daughter was part of this."

"Don't worry so much," China said.

"Easy for you to say," Rick said, chucking her under the chin. "You can't lose your job over this."

"Sure I can," China said. "I can even be deported."

"Deported?" Rick's eyes darted from one girl to the other, not sure if he believed them.

The girls laughed. Deedee nodded. "It's true. She could. Back to Guatemala."

China stirred the boiling spaghetti noodles one more time, smashing one against the side of the pot. "I think they're ready, Rick."

"So?" he teased.

"I thought you wanted to take them off the fire. You know, all that macho stuff about being strong and manly . . ."

"Fine. You do it if you think you're so strong."

"Okay." China took the industrial pot holders from

the hook on the wall and grabbed the handles. Rick stood to one side, his arms crossed, a smirk across his face. John stuck his head around the corner. Deedee watched Rick.

Without much effort, China lifted the huge pot and walked it to the sink where she poured off most of the boiling water. Then she added a bucket of ice, stirred it around, then poured off the liquid again. She looked up at Rick, triumphant, and saw Rick's jaw hanging open. Deedee watched him, her hand covering her laugh. John's face registered no emotion.

Rick walked over to China. "Lemme see those biceps, Amazon Woman!" He grabbed hold of her upper arms and squeezed like he was checking oranges for juice content. "You'd never know these worked so well. Very little observable muscle, yet quite capable."

"Thank you, Arnold Schwarzenegger, for your expert opinion."

"Men are always stronger than women," John commented coolly.

China put her hands on her hips. "Not always."

"For example, no woman can beat me in an arm wrestling match." John pushed up his T-shirt sleeve and flexed his muscle.

China and Deedee exchanged looks.

"We can," Deedee piped up.

We? thought China. *She couldn't even wrestle my grandma.*

"Okay," John said, grabbing two stools and pushing them to the prep table. "Duel."

Rick smacked his hands together. "This oughta be good."

Deedee straddled the stool. "Me first." She turned to wink at a confused China and put her right elbow on the steel table.

John flexed his arm again, felt it, then sat on his stool, elbow on the table. He flexed his fingers, then slowly latched onto Deedee's hand.

"We're holding hands!" Deedee cooed in a fake Heather-type voice. John blushed.

Rick stood with his feet spread apart, arms resting on the table. "On your mark, get set, go!"

With one swift push, Deedee's hand lay flat on the table. She sighed deeply. "I guess you win."

John smiled. "Of course I do. No woman is a match for a man's strength. Next?"

Deedee moved so China could take her place. China concentrated on doing the right things—not on her opponent or on winning. She positioned her elbow on the table and made sure her arm was straight as she gripped John's hand.

"What are you trying to do?" he sneered. "Are you pretending you're in Petaluma for the finals?"

China ignored him, concentrating on her grip and position.

At Rick's "Go!" she readied her muscles for a locked position. So when John tried to fell her as he did

Deedee, he met a brick wall of resistance. As the seconds passed, John could not get China's arm to move out of place more than an inch or two. China knew when her muscles were ready to push. When the blood had poured in, strengthening and tightening them, she looked at her goal, staring at the spot on the prep table where she imagined her hand needed to go. As she concentrated, she began a slow movement forward, never considering his resistance or strength, only the goal.

Slowly it approached. And then, without a sound, the back of John's hand touched the steel and stayed there.

In a flash, he jumped from his stool. Rick and Deedee cheered, Deedee holding China's right arm in the air.

"She cheated!" John screamed, humiliation coloring his face beet red.

"She did not!" Rick said firmly. "I watched very carefully."

"She did! She had to! No girl can . . ."

"Face it," Rick teased. "You're a wimp."

John spun to face China. "You'll pay," he promised.

China turned away so he wouldn't see her laugh. He stomped away and they could hear him slamming pots in the back sink.

"He'll get over it in about 10 minutes," Rick predicted, looking at his watch. "He always does. I tease him that it's his Irish temper. That makes him even madder."

"Why?" Deedee asked.

"Because he's from Columbia," Rick said.

"You're mean," China said.

Rick grabbed a couple of spaghetti strands and threw them at her. China stood there, her hands on her hips, spaghetti coiled and stuck to her hair. "No more food fights."

"Can't handle them, huh?" Rick teased.

"Not the way you play." China looked at Deedee, who winked at her.

China whipped her head back and forth, the spaghetti getting tangled in her hair, rather than flying off as she expected. The dog barked and barked, staring at her head.

China knelt down next to him. "What is it, little guy? Don't you like my hair flying all over the place?"

The dog leaped at her, his open jaws aiming for her ear. China covered her face, while Deedee shouted a worthless "No!" He fell backwards, his lips smacking over the spaghetti.

"He likes spaghetti!" Rick shouted, as he grabbed a couple more strands, and dangled them in front of the dog's eyes. The dog's floppy ears perked up, his eyes and nose following the jiggling worms. Rick tossed them in the air. Nothing happened. In unison, they all looked up. The spaghetti had stuck to the ceiling.

"Pretty designs," Deedee observed.

"I suppose I'll be elected to get it down," China said,

sitting cross-legged on the floor, staring at the ceiling.

The little dog stood underneath the strands and began to bark furiously. Each bark lifted his whole body off the ground. Gravity began to lure the spaghetti off the ceiling, uncoiling it until it hung by its tip. When it dropped, the dog was ready, catching it in his jaws.

"That was too cool," Rick laughed. "We've got to try it again." This time, he threw one piece up in the air, hard. The dog barked and barked until it came down and he devoured it.

"My turn!" China said, choosing an extra-long strand. Only half of it stuck, and the dog had his treat without much effort.

Deedee grabbed a piece of cheese from the lunch sandwich leftovers. She heaved it into the air, hitting the ceiling, but it came right back down.

"Too greasy," China noted.

Rick took a few pieces of bologna, cut them in half, then threw one-half into the air. "Bingo!" he said when it stuck.

The dog went nuts. He stood on his hind legs and hopped until he fell over in the direction where his tilt usually led him. He tried again, barking like mad, trying to hop on his hind feet. He was so busy spinning and dancing that he missed the bologna when it fell. He pounced on it, devouring it, saliva spitting everywhere.

The trio laughed until they cried. "Again!" Deedee

jumped and clapped like a little kid.

Rick tossed another piece, which held on. The dog danced a jig, panting, squealing, and barking.

"Go, bologna!" Deedee shouted.

"Bologna . . . Bologna . . ." the girls chanted together. Rick clapped his hands in time, until the meat fell and disappeared into hungry jaws.

"Good, Bologna!" Rick said, patting the dog on the head.

Deedee and China looked at each other. "Bologna," they both said at the same time.

China dangled a piece of meat over the dog's head. "Get it, Bologna!" she encouraged. The dog shivered and danced again.

"That dog is crazy for the stuff," Rick commented.

"So we christen him Bologna," China announced.

"Here! Here!" agreed Deedee, who held high a glass of grape punch.

For the rest of the afternoon they tried out different foods to see what Bologna would like.

Rick always found the foods that made them laugh. John, who had finally quit pouting, gently held open Bologna's jaws, while Rick squirted his mouth full of whipped cream. When John let the dog's jaws snap shut, he shrieked, "Blizzard!" while whipped cream flew everywhere. Bologna licked his chops and barked for more.

"Enough!" China said after the fourth time. "You'll make him sick."

"You want him fattened up, don't you?" John asked.

"Yeah, but with good food."

"Okay," Rick said, "how about this?" He produced a large can of peanut butter. He scooped some out with his finger and had John hold open Bologna's jaws. With a quick swipe, he smeared the peanut butter on the roof of Bologna's mouth. The happy dog licked and licked and licked, his pink tongue darting in and out. For five minutes he imitated a curious snake with a determined tongue.

"I don't know about this, guys," China said.

"The dog is happy," Rick said.

"He likes it," John said. "Just look at his face. He doesn't run away when we bring out the peanut butter. Watch."

John held the can of peanut butter where Bologna could see it. He ran straight over to John, panting happily.

Deedee rested her elbow on China's shoulder. "He seems to enjoy it as much as we do, China. I know it seems like it could be mean. But I think we need to just make sure he isn't running away from anything or resisting. Then it would definitely be out of bounds."

"I guess."

Deedee reluctantly left for her boat shack job, and the rest of the crew focused more of their attention on dinner preparations than the dog. China found a quiet corner that made a good hiding spot, lined it with towels, and encouraged Bologna to take a nap. He eagerly nosed the towels until it made a suitable bed and lay down, intent on taking a nap.

Between jobs, China tiptoed to the corner and looked at her baby. In her heart, she knew she should be talking to Mr. Kiersey, or at least Magda, about the dog. But she couldn't bear to give him up. And each moment her fear grew a little larger, knowing her world would blow apart the minute they discovered the bundle of flesh-and-blood contraband.

CHAPTER NINE

THURSDAY MORNING, CHINA AND DEEDEE took the little kids' book *Frog and Toad Together* to read to Magda. China read the Frog parts, and Deedee read the Toad parts.

Magda sat hunched over in the big green chair. Her whole body shuddered with laughter, her flesh quivering in ripples.

When the girls finished, and Magda had stopped laughing, her flesh seemed to sag.

"You know," she said to the girls, her voice quivering, "I could almost swear my body is poisoning itself."

The girls looked at each other, their eyes wide and questioning. "Please let me tell Dad," Deedee begged. "You've been sick for four days now."

"Three and a half," Magda corrected. "Not long for the flu."

"But you just said . . ." China stated.

Magda looked at them, her eyes rheumy, but full of

fire. "I shouldn't have said anything. It could be a strange form of flu. But . . ." she wagged her head, her flattened salt-and-pepper hair sticking to her scalp.

The girls waited for her to talk some more. "If my suspicions are right . . ." she wagged her head again, covering her eyes with her hand. "Oh, I do hope I'm wrong. It would be so painful to be right."

China went over to Magda's chair and perched on the overstuffed arm. She took Magda's hand in hers and held it. And waited.

"Remember how Heather was so awful to you?" Magda said, looking up at China, her eyes begging for understanding.

"How could I ever forget?" China interrupted.

"Yet I kept telling you that the poor girl had some deep, deep inside hurt that made her act like that? We needed to love her and do what was right, no matter how awful she was."

China nodded. "I hated that. I'd rather be mean right back."

"You were," Deedee softly reminded her.

China stuck her tongue out at her.

"If I told you I needed your help, I know you would automatically hate someone, and I don't want that. But I can't do this on my own."

The girls nodded, looking at her.

"The first thing I want you to know is that there are people in this world with hurts far deeper than you can imagine. Hurts that can twist how they look at the world and how they treat other people. Because of some very crazy, out-of-control thing that happened sometime in the past, they in turn try to control every situation and every person to make their own life go the way they want it. In their own minds, they feel they are totally right, and that justifies their actions.

"I'm not saying the bad things that have happened in their lives make their mean actions okay or right. But knowing their past might make a difference in how we treat them. Am I making sense?"

The girls nodded. "It's so hard to be nice to someone who does horrible things," Deedee said.

"But looking at them with God's eyes can give us an understanding we couldn't otherwise have. You see, it is only by trusting God and His grace that we can choose the right way to behave when horrible things happen to us. Every time we are stuck in the pit of a deeply hurting place, we have a choice to turn to God or turn toward bitterness."

"So why this big lecture?" Deedee asked.

"If my hunch is right, then we have someone at camp who was deeply hurt and ran toward bitterness rather than toward God. Sometimes those hurts make them think they have to control everything rather than let God call the shots."

"Who is it?" Deedee asked.

"I won't say. I told you all this because I want you to have the eyes of God rather than the eyes of someone who only saw Queen Heather and not the hurting

Heather behind the nasty actions." Magda took her free hand and patted China's.

As Magda took a deep breath, all her stomachs and breasts moved as one. "I want you to sneak me out some food without anyone in the kitchen knowing."

China tilted her head. "But Rick makes you whatever you want every day."

"I want him to keep making me the food, but I want you to sneak me out a small portion of whatever the rest of the camp kids are eating."

"Why?"

"Please don't ask, and don't tell anyone else. I feel really foolish asking you to do this anyway. So please understand this might just be a foolish old woman talking."

"What do you think Rick is doing?" China demanded.

"Did I say any names, China honey? I don't want you walking around that place putting up walls over something you don't know all the facts about. Understand?"

China nodded.

When the girls left, Deedee said, "What do you think is happening?"

China slowly shook her head. "I don't know. But I would guess she's got to be talking about Rick, no matter what she says."

"I want to talk to my dad."

"Deedee," China snapped. "Your dad is not King of

Everything. He isn't God. He can't make everything happen."

"What?"

"Every time something happens, you always want to run straight to your dad. Why don't you ever let people work out problems the way they want to?"

"Because my dad is wise. He's dealt with all kinds of problems throughout the years. It's part of his job." Deedee had tears in her eyes. "I thought you liked my dad."

"I do. It's just that you can't seem to do anything on your own. You run to Daddy for every little thing."

"No, I don't."

"You want to, though."

"What's wrong with wanting to?" Deedee asked.

China sighed. "I'm sorry. Maybe I actually miss my own dad. Or wish he could be more like yours. Maybe I've been on my own in a foreign country too much, so it's taught me to be more independent. I can't go to my dad for every little thing. He's gone so much. We can't call him since there are no phones in most of the remote Indian villages. We don't see him for a week at a time. Then we see him for two; then we don't for a month. I can't count on him. So I've learned to do it myself."

They walked the rest of the way to the kitchen in silence. "Girls," a huge voice boomed from inside the screen door. "I've been waiting for you." Kemper pushed open the door. "I need your help." He handed Deedee a list.

"Sardines, red Jell-o, peanut butter, and syrup," Deedee read out loud. "Is this some kind of bizarre snack?"

Kemper's deep brown eyes got that crazy look of fiendish delight.

"He's got a new game up his sleeve," China said. "Look at that face."

Kemper's mustache jumped. "It's a doozy. You're gonna love it."

"Uh-oh," Deedee said, backing away. "This means we're gonna be grossed out."

Kemper wagged his head, "Ahh, you girls know me too well." He smacked his large hands together. "This one's called Twisted Twister . . . not to be confused with any rock group by similar names."

"Maybe we should call it Twisted Mister—after your brilliant mind, of course," China suggested.

"Brilliant mind?" Kemper said thoughtfully, pulling his ever-present pencil from the wad of curly hair over his ear. It was the only patch on his head longer than a nub. "How's this for brilliance? Actually, I got this one from my friend Paul."

"Go on, Kemper," Deedee prodded. "Time's wasting."

"We have one Twister mat for each team. You know, with the colored spots. One row of green, one of blue, one yellow, and one red. Each team sends one player to each Twister mat."

"So you have five players from different teams at

each mat," China clarified.

"Correct. Then you play Twister."

"So?" Deedee remarked. "What's so twisted about that?"

Kemper grinned. "Well, there's a pie pan of red Jell-o on each of the red circles, a pie pan of stinky sardines on all the green circles . . ."

"And pie pans of peanut butter and syrup on the other colors," China said, shaking her head in disbelief. "You were right, Deedee. I am grossed out."

"I told you," Deedee said. "The man thrives on gross."

Kemper glanced at his watch. "I need to run. But you girls get to make the pans of all this junk and bring it to me at the battlefield in 20 minutes. Can do?"

"Can do," China said, sighing.

Kemper left, and the girls went to work. In between filling pans, they tossed Bologna a hunk of Jell-o and gave him some peanut butter to lick. China dabbed a dot of syrup on the end of his nose for a treat and left him a sardine, which he sniffed once and ignored for the rest of the time they worked.

Rick walked around them, his face dark and unhappy. The more the girls laughed and groaned over the contents of the smelly pie tins, the more the cloud over him seemed to grow.

Deedee left, pushing the first cart of pie pans. China wanted to say hello to Rick and wash her hands before she went. She skipped up to him, a sardine dangling from her fingers. "Look, Rick, a snack," China said, trying to cheer him up.

"Quit playing with the food," Rick snapped. "We don't have it to waste you know."

China stared at him.

"What're you staring at?" he shouted.

"You," China said softly. "What's the problem?"

"There is no problem, except you and your giggly friend. This is a place of employment, not a place to play games."

"We're helping Kemper," she explained.

"Yeah, always willing to help Kemper, but never willing to help me."

"Do you need help, Rick?" China asked, tossing the sardine in a trash barrel.

"Yes, I do. But you never seem willing. You are always too busy with the dog or with your hoity-toity important friend. But you won't have time to help me."

"I thought this was a job, Rick," China explained. "Regular hours, regular pay."

"A truly caring worker, a true *Christian*, would not be such a stickler about hours and pay. They give." Rick sounded like he mimicked someone else, his voice sarcastic and high-pitched. "They sacrifice what they want for the good of their fellow Christians. Didn't Jesus sacrifice everything to be with others and serve them? Well, if you claim to be such a good Christian, I'd like to see some actual fruit of the vine here."

"Okay," China answered. "I'll try to help out more."

John came barrelling out of the walk-in, shoving a loaded cart ahead of him. The cart slammed into the security handle inside the door.

"Be careful," Rick shouted. "That's the third time you've hit it today. It's going to break."

"Lay off," John retorted. "I'm more loyal to you than she is, and you treat me like this?"

"Enough!" roared Rick.

China forgot about washing her hands and grabbed her cart and left.

All the way to the battlefield, China moved through the thoughts cluttering her mind. It was like trying to walk through her bedroom at home. Thoughts scattered about like clothes she didn't bother to put away. Like papers in piles around her room. Standing in the doorway, she could never get through all those clothes, all those papers, all those thoughts. They were a jumbled mess. But stepping in, she chose one piece of clothing, one thought, looked at it and put it away.

Why is Rick mad at me?

Maybe he's not mad at me. Maybe he's stressed without Magda there. Maybe he's not used to the long, hard hours the kitchen cook must put in. Maybe he and John were fighting over something again. She'd seen little spats before but didn't think much about them.

China thought about how she could help. When she felt stressed but couldn't really change anything, one thing always made her feel better. Chocolate.

After the crazy twister game, when toes were full of slimy, gooey, stinky stuff, China and Deedee gathered up the mushed pans, piled them on their carts and started back to the kitchen. When they got there, Rick was nowhere in sight. Bologna raced up to them and licked their hands, sniffing wildly at the pie tins.

They each tossed a quarter-moon of bologna on the ceiling to watch the little dog dance, then kissed him and made him stay behind. His little whiskered face tilted one way, then the other, as they left.

"After lunch I want to come in and help Rick," China told Deedee.

"You aren't scheduled until 3:00, are you?"

China shook her head. "Rick seemed a little stressed. Maybe one of his workers didn't show up. I think it might help him if I came in early."

"I was hoping you'd help me think of some crazy stunt to pull on the lifeguards. I want to get back at them for all the fake bugs and junk they leave around for me."

"Maybe tonight."

After lunch, China bought a Cookies N' Mint Hershey's Bar and Reese's Peanut Butter Cups. She showed them to John. "To soothe Rick's spirit and bring life to his anguished soul," she intoned, bowing with a flourish.

John stared at her, his eyes turning a muddy brown. "You are the rudest, most cruel person I have ever met."

China backed away, unsure of what she'd done. Bologna stood between the two of them and barked up at John. "What did I do?" China asked, totally confused.

"How dare you. Are you trying to kill my friend?" he hissed, as he slowly moved toward her.

China backed away at the same pace that John moved toward her. Bologna kept his behind at China's legs, still barking at John. "I . . . I . . . " China said helplessly.

"You know Rick's a diabetic. You know how hard he fights temptation. You know how much he loves chocolate. But you bring it anyway, saying how nice you're trying to be."

Bologna snarled and barked louder.

"Shut up!" John yelled at the dog. Bologna kept up his vigil. "Shut up! I told you." With one swift move, John's foot caught Bologna underneath his belly, lifted him, and made him fly a few feet. "Stupid dog. As stupid as his master." John spun around and marched off to the ovens, opening doors and slamming them shut again.

China picked up Bologna and ran outside, holding her sobs until she got there. Behind Eelapuash, in the shade of the building and clustered pine trees, China cried and cried, checking Bologna all over for damage. He licked her face and wagged his tail as though nothing had happened.

China sat outside, shaking, not knowing what to

do. *He's having a bad day*, she kept telling herself. *He's having a bad day, and I made it worse.* She held Bologna until he squirmed to get away and play in the dirt. He chased a feather, then came back and sat in front of her.

"Bologna," China said softly, "I think I'm going crazy."

CHAPTER TEN

CHINA LOOKED AT HER WATCH and knew she couldn't put off the inevitable any longer. She stood, brushed off the seat of her pants, and wiggled her fingers at Bologna. He trotted to her at a tilt, then stayed by her ankles as she went back into the kitchen.

Rick moved about the kitchen. He wasn't slamming things around. Nor was he singing. He looked at China and calmly asked, "Are you here to work?"

China nodded. "Where's John?"

"In the back."

"He . . ."

"Everyone has a bad day now and then," Rick said.

China nodded again.

Nothing more was said. China hoped for the apology that never came. He was her superior. He was her authority. She couldn't tell him she thought he owed her one. She wasn't sure his comment about bad days wasn't an apology.

Work passed slowly and quietly. Rick calmly gave

directions; China obeyed them. When John walked by, he always found something that didn't seem quite right. He didn't like the size scoop she used to dole out butter in little pleated paper bowls. He didn't like her putting yellow corn in yellow dishes. He wanted them in the green ones. He didn't say anything cruel. Nothing derogatory. But nothing she did was right. Bologna stayed at her heels most of the time, careful to stay out of John's way.

Deedee met China at 8:00 when she got off work. China stared after Bologna, wanting so badly to take him with her, frightened that John would hurt him. But Rick was in the shadows, cooing and talking to Bologna. She didn't have a place for Bologna. Not yet. So she would have to trust the dog with Rick.

"Here," Deedee said, shoving two envelopes into China's hand. "One's from your mom and one's from your aunt."

"Isn't it awful?" China said as she turned the top letter over and over in her hand. "I feel almost like I don't know these people. Like they don't exist."

"I'm used to people coming in and out of my life so fast that I really don't think of much beyond this camp anyway."

"What makes me even more awful," China continued, "is that I don't even miss them. I am so glad to be away from home, that I forget I'm supposed to care."

"Don't you miss them at all?"

China went over the mental images she had of her

family. "You can have Cam any day of the week. Older brothers with a brain made for studying are totally obnoxious. Nic would be cute if he didn't spend his life eating and zooming matchbox cars over everything. Mom. Well, she irritates me to no end. People keep telling me I'll get over it in a few years. It's just a phase. Phase or no phase, I'd rather live far away from her than in the same house."

"And we already know about your dad."

"Yeah."

"Isn't there anything you miss about Guatemala?"

China smiled, closing her eyes. "It's so green there. Everything is wildly, passionately green. Orchids grow on the trees, the most beautiful parasites you'll ever see. The Quetzal bird has a tail that's probably four times as long as he is. I miss the daily rainstorms. You can see them come from a long way off and we all place a guess as to how long it will take them to get to us. I got to be the best guesser. I miss the volcanos and the hot spots under the bed that are perfect for drying sweaters, nylons, and making bread rise."

"Read your letter."

Dear China,
We've had quite a week here. It's amazing how much can happen in one week.

China looked at Deedee. "I have no clue what she's talking about, do you?"

"None, whatsoever," Deedee replied in the same sarcastic tone.

> *Dad was off in the village of Cobán doing his usual thing. I expected him back on Thursday, the same day I talked to you. I didn't worry much when he was late. Actually I didn't even think about him being late until I woke Friday morning and he still wasn't here. Nic came running into the house saying the pan cart wasn't there. Instead, there were soldiers all over. Cam had his book bag dangling from his back as he finished off his coffee. He shrugged his shoulders and commented, "Someone is probably trying to overthrow the government again." He stood up and started out the door. I asked him if he thought it was wise to go to the library today and he said he figured that was the safest place to be.*
>
> *Nic started to get scared. I was already worried about Dad and notified the office that he hadn't returned. I hate these takeovers. I know they are common in small countries like this. But I've never gotten used to them like Cam has.*

China shivered. "I hate them too, Deedee. You come out of a store and soldiers are hanging around with machine guns. Sometimes they glare at you. It's spooky."

"I think I'll take my mountains with bears and

mountain lions over machine guns any day."

Anyway, I didn't know if I should stay home and wait for Dad or if I should continue to the market. Nic was terrified to leave the house, so we stayed home. All morning he lay by the front gate and peered outside very carefully. In the afternoon, he was in the backyard with soldiers lined up and marching down his own imaginary street.

Dad still wasn't home by nightfall, and I wondered if the guerrillas got him and he was being held somewhere. I tried not to panic and spent an awful lot of time praying. I always feel guilty that when times are tough, I pray every second. When times are going well, I pray throughout the day, but not about and for everything. God isn't first on my mind until worry sets in.

Cam didn't show up until 8:00. I had begun to pray for his safety, too. Turns out he did his usual studying, forgetting to watch the time until they kicked him out of the library. Then the buses weren't running, so he had to walk all the way home.

Dad strolled in about 10:15 on Saturday morning. Word of the takeover had drifted to the village before it happened. So he hung out until he knew it was safe to travel. I wish we had beepers here. It would make life much easier. Not that Dad could call from the villages anyway.

I'm glad you're safe and probably having fun.
If you change your mind, or if you and Deedee
don't get along, you know Aunt Liddy would love
to have you. I pray for you, too.
      Love, Mom

China folded the letter and put it back in the light-weight airmail envelope. "I'm glad I didn't know about my dad until now."

Deedee nodded. "Does it make you want to go back, to be with them and stuff?"

China shook her head so emphatically her hair whipped the air. "No way. It makes me even more glad I'm not there. It also makes me want to go to the campfire tonight."

"Me, too."

China read the short, nice note from her Aunt Liddy. Her aunt apologized again for jumping to conclusions the week before. "I hope you will forgive me and that we can start new with our friendship," the note said. It made China smile. She couldn't say no to someone like that. She appreciated any adult who could make a mistake around a kid and then admit it.

The flames of the campfire crackled and spit sparks into the cool night air. A bright, thin moon hung low in the sky. Low enough to not disturb the stars. China and Deedee both put sweatshirts on, then lay back on the sandy beach to get lost in the wild scattering of stars and listen to the lake lap at the shore between songs.

Christopher and Randy Fong each played guitar while the kids sang songs that had to go straight from their mouths to God's ears. "As the Deer"; "I Love You, Lord"; the new "Jesus Loves Me."

The voices of the campers were cotton-soft in the night air. You could rest a tired heart on them. A hurting one. God seemed close enough to touch.

China raised up on one arm to watch the fire. Sparks popped into the air, breaking free from the main fire, only to disintegrate in a second. Kemper sat near the fire, watching the musicians lead worship. The orange glow reflected off the eternal layer of sweat on his black skin. A hint of a smile touched his face. Eyes closed, his body swayed gently with the rhythm of the music. His palms faced the stars. Not in a proud gesture for the world to see. A humble gesture. One that was almost hidden in the dark. *He's sharing the company of a friend*, China thought, wondering at something she could see but couldn't describe.

Her gaze shifted, not wanting to intrude on his private, silent conversation. She scanned the group, half wishing she could be a camper again. And again and again. There was something here that touched and completed her deep inside. Something that watered the garden within and made it grow.

Her eyes stopped on a lone figure off to one side. Her heart skipped. *What is Rick doing here?* She watched him, his face just out of reach of the flickering orange firelight. His curled hand rested on his lap. He didn't sing. But he watched intently. Whenever a camper shared something touching, he leaned forward, straining to hear. He nodded when one kid talked about how he had felt so left out until he came to camp. He made friends. But mostly, he'd found that he really was someone important to God. When the girl China knew as Juanita shared how excited she was that she and her best friend had developed a closer relationship to God and to each other, she thought he wiped away a tear. And when the singing began again, he turned his face away, leaning back on the rock that was his chair.

I wish I could figure him out. I wish I knew what I could do to make him happy.

Be his friend, came the quiet answer.

China sat up and hugged her knees to her chest, never taking her eyes off him. She felt Deedee sit up next to her. "What?" Deedee whispered.

At that moment, Rick turned toward them, his face looking full into China's over the fire. He forced a weak smile, then turned his head down and away.

"You make him blush," Deedee said.

"You can't see that," China said, blushing herself.

"Body language, China. Watch his body language."

"I *do,*" China said, frustrated.

"So why don't you ever get it right? Why don't you see what everyone else does?"

China put her face in her hands. *Why don't I ever get it right? What is right?* "What does everyone else see?" China looked at Deedee.

"That he obviously likes you."

"So you are telling me that he's acting the way guys always do when they like you. This is normal?"

"YES."

Two people turned around and glared at them. "SHHH!"

"I'm so confused," China admitted. "Maybe I'm not ready for this because I don't get it."

Deedee shrugged her shoulders and turned her attention toward the front. "Maybe not. Because you've certainly been acting strange lately. Not the fun, energetic China I knew last week."

China's mind faced the challenge, derailed a moment, then caught onto tenth gear. "After campfire we'll just have to change that, won't we?"

Deedee's green eyes swept over China's face. "Oh, no. I've really created a monster this time, haven't I?"

China just smiled.

When the last note of singing had died away and the last prayers of commitment and thanks had been said, the kids stood in small groups talking, laughing, and tossing objects into the fire to see how they'd burn. China nudged Deedee. "You said you wanted to get the lifeguards."

Deedee's eyes brightened. "Yeah? You have an idea?"

"It depends. What kind of floor do they have in their cabin?"

"Lifeguards get cement because they track in too much sand and water. The rest of the staff gets carpet. There's a cabin for the three girl lifeguards, who I fondly call the Lifeguardettes, and one for the five guys."

"Perfect. Will they know we did it?"

"I doubt it. They think I'm sweet and innocent. Actually, they play games on each other so often they'll think the other half of the group did it."

"Hah!"

"So what do we do?"

"Lifeguards love the water, right?"

"Yeah."

China smiled deviously. "We're going to give them all they could wish for."

Deedee led the way through the back shortcuts, avoiding trails as much as possible. At the new maintenance shed, Deedee climbed through the window, then came out the door with a garden hose. When they neared the guys' cabin, they collected a garbage can and lifted out and tied the plastic trash bag.

Twenty feet away from the cabin they hooked up the hose to a water spigot and put the nozzle near the bottom of the garbage can. When the water covered the nozzle, they turned on the water full force until the garbage can was full.

"I can hardly move this," Deedee hissed.

"Grab one handle with both hands."

The girls each took a handle and pulled with all their might. The water sloshed out of the can and drenched them from the waist down. "Keep pulling," China whispered.

At the cabin, the girls tilted the garbage can until it rested on the door. Then they ran to the cover of the trees, mapping out their way of escape.

"Now what?" Deedee asked.

"We have a choice. We either wait, hoping they'll come out; we leave and get wind of what happened tomorrow; or we make them come out so we can watch for ourselves."

Deedee wrung her hands together. "Oh, I have to see this."

"You ready to run?"

"You bet."

"You'll have to lead," China reminded her.

"Trust me."

The girls picked up pebbles and began to throw them at the side cabin window. "Hey, Eagle!" came a muffled voice from inside the cabin. "I think your secret admirer is waiting for you."

"Tell her to go away," a voice answered. "She's too young."

"You tell her," the first voice answered.

The girls sent more pebbles fast and furious.

"Whoever is out there" came another voice, "is not alone."

"Fine. I'll check it out."

The girls ran to the front of the cabin where they could watch the action.

The door opened with a jerk. Light spilled out into the night. The garbage can lurched toward Eagle. He tried to catch it, but even his muscles were no match for the momentum of surging water. Like a tidal wave, it poured into the cabin. Four faces looked cartoonish with gaping mouths, wide astonished eyes, and water spilling around their ankles.

"I thought you said there were five," China said.

Deedee shrugged her shoulders, her hand over her mouth, her cheeks ballooned with stifled laughter.

After a long pause, the four cartoons moved into action. A fifth body came around the door.

"Let's go!" China whispered.

As the girls hoped, the five lifeguards ran in the direction of the pebbles. China and Deedee ran in the opposite direction.

"So what do we do for the female batch?" Deedee asked.

"That's tomorrow night," China answered. "We'll need more supplies for them."

CHAPTER ELEVEN

WHEN THE GIRLS REACHED HOME, China found a small, white bag filled with sugarless candy on her pillow.

"How do you rate?" Deedee asked, her bottom lip poking out.

"I paid your mother to get it for me when she went down the hill today."

"So do I get any?" Deedee asked.

"Nope. Sorry. They're a peace offering."

The next morning when Deedee and China took Magda her breakfast, instead of a lump buried under quilts, they saw a weak but improved woman sitting in her chair.

"You look better," China said, kissing Magda's cheek.

"I am better."

"So your hunch was right?" Deedee asked.

"Maybe," Magda said.

"How're you going to know for sure?"

Magda's whole body sighed. "I don't know."

"Do you know who it is?" China asked, eager to know which person in the kitchen she should personally strangle.

Magda sighed again, turning toward her wearily. "No."

"Is there anything we can do?" China asked.

"I could talk to my . . ." Deedee stopped midsentence casting a glance in China's direction.

Magda shook her head. "I guess the only thing you can do is keep your eyes open, China. And some meal soon I'll be brave enough to try the special meal Rick has cooked to see if I get sick again."

A short time later, China trotted into the kitchen with Deedee at her heels. Bologna galloped toward them, whimpering his excitement. Both girls squatted on the ground, and immediately were attacked by a bouncing fur ball with a wildly lapping tongue.

"Well, it's the best friends," Rick said, his arms crossed.

China looked into Rick's eyes and again saw the silliness mixed with something else. Something distant, sad, and maybe even angry. She reached into her pocket and pulled out a small white bag. She held it up to him. "Peace offering."

"Peace offering?"

"Well, I only wanted to cheer you up yesterday when I brought the chocolate . . ."

"What chocolate?" Rick opened the bag and peered inside. He took a wrapped green candy from the bag.

"This isn't chocolate."

"No, John told me you're diabetic. I didn't know that, so I got you some sugarless candy instead. I don't know if they make sugarless chocolate that would taste any good . . ."

"John told you I'm diabetic?"

"Yeah, he took the candy bars and threw them away; he didn't want you to see them." China stroked Bologna's ears while Deedee stroked his body.

"You brought me chocolate yesterday."

China couldn't figure out the tone of his flat voice. "Yeah. I'm really sorry."

"Why should you be sorry?"

"Because I didn't know chocolate is such a temptation for you."

"Did you by any chance happen to bring a Cookies N' Mint and a Reese's Peanut Butter Cups?"

China looked at the dog, embarrassed. "Yeah."

Rick leaned back against the prep table. He looked over his shoulder. "John?" he called. He opened the walk-in and looked in. "John, come out here a sec."

John pushed a cart piled high with crates of lettuce, tomatoes, onions, and cheese blocks through the door, again ramming the security handle. "Man," he muttered angrily, moving around the cart to get the handle unjammed. "This stupid handle is always in the way."

"Not for long the way you keep ramming it, John. If you'd just go slower."

"Yeah, yeah. What do you want, Rick? I'm real busy here." John looked down, noticing the girls on the floor with the dog. "Oh, look. It's the Siamese twins and the health hazard," he said with a twisted smile.

"John," Rick said, diverting his attention from the girls. "Hysterical joke you pulled yesterday."

"Yeah? Which one."

"The one where you told China that I'm diabetic."

John's face clouded over. "I didn't do any such thing. You're not diabetic, so why would I say that?"

Rick crossed his arms over his chest. "For a dumb joke, I guess. And I also suppose I have to take back the thanks I gave you for the chocolate I thought you got me. 'Twas a loverly thought, anyway." Rick moved away, singing about chocolate from "Loverly" in a fake Liza Doolittle voice.

John stared at China. "Diabetic?" He shook his head. He looked around and as Rick disappeared from around the corner, he hissed, "Why don't you just leave poor Rick alone. He's got a lot of stress from working to cover Magda's absence. I'm here to put in extra hours. If you're not here to do the same, maybe you aren't really committed to making sure things go well."

He pushed the cart past the girls to the prep table and began to unload the produce. Rick came back around the corner, a large tray in his mitted hand. "Look girls, either stay and work, or get out of the way."

China and Deedee looked at each other. China gathered Bologna in her arms, and they took off out the door.

"Sheesh," Deedee said, looking over her shoulder at the kitchen, then back at China. "What's got into them?"

"Who knows? But they're both becoming a real joy to be around." China put Bologna on the ground, snapping his leash to his collar. "Let's get out of here."

"Where to?" Deedee asked. "The falls? You haven't been there yet."

China shook her head. "The store."

"Again?"

"We need water balloons. Do you think they have them?"

"I suppose. They seem to have at least one of everything else."

The store was dark and cool. Another world of worn, wood floors. China always felt like she should be tying her horse up at the hitching post outside. In her mind, she heard spurs jingle as she walked. One section of the store had junk toys for kids. Plastic gadgets, guns, soldiers, and balls that were guaranteed to break within 15 minutes of play. They found the balloons between the party supplies and the u-break-um toys.

"One bag or two?" Deedee asked.

"We'll only have enough time for five or six apiece, so one bag's enough."

On the way back to camp, the girls hiked down to the creek. China ripped a strand of beef jerky off the piece Deedee offered. Bologna sat, wagging his tail in the dirt, happily waiting for his turn. China popped the beef in her mouth, chewing slowly. She patted Bologna on the head, who proceeded to wag his tail even harder. "Does this bother you?" she asked Deedee.

"What?" Deedee grabbed a handful of her long curly hair, lifting it off her neck and holding it in the air to let the breeze cool her off.

"Hiding Bologna."

Deedee put her head down on her knees, her response muffled. "I'm getting tired of it."

China looked through the trees at the creek racing beside them. "I feel like life is going on all around us and we're missing out. We can't help Kemper much."

"We can't go on the slide."

"We can't go on the Blob."

Deedee's head popped up. "I feel totally guilty."

"That too."

"So when do we tell? What do we do?" Deedee asked.

"I think we should have a plan first."

"Agreed. But what?"

China pulled off her shoes and socks, jamming her feet into the icy creek water. Bologna stood at the edge of the water, listing to the right, and leaned over to lap at the fast-moving water.

Deedee scooted closer to a boulder and leaned

against it. She picked up rocks and tossed them into the creek one at a time. "I can make a song with different sized rocks, China, listen."

Deedee gathered many sizes of rocks and set them into piles of similar shape and size. She tested the sound each made as it hit the water, then thought a few moments.

Plipp, plunk, plink, plunk, plipp, plipp, plipp.

China tried not to laugh at Deedee's earnest face— her mouth puckered and twisted to one side. When Deedee finished, her face relaxed and her eyes danced. "So! Which song?"

"'Mary Had a Little Lamb,'" China guessed.

"Got it!"

"Very good. Now can you use that mind of yours to get us out of this predicament?"

"I thought that was your job," Deedee replied. "You're the one who thinks up all the good stuff to do to other people."

China fluttered her feet in the water. "Yeah, my mind can think up bizarre things, but it's not real great when it comes to practicality."

"And mine is?"

"You're right," China agreed solemnly, "I forgot your brain doesn't work too well at all."

In a flash, Deedee moved forward, cupped her hand in the water, and flung a handful at China.

"You creep!" China yelled, kicking water back at Deedee.

Deedee's hand moved fast and furious, flinging water at China as fast as she could. China's feet returned the favor while Bologna barked, his body bouncing up and down. He looked from one soggy person to the other, not knowing which one he should focus his warnings upon.

When both girls were thoroughly soaked and shivering, they lay back in the sun. Bologna curled up between them, occasionally licking the water that dripped from their clothing.

When the sun had baked their clothes half-dry, Deedee spoke. "You're going to hate me for this."

"I already hate you for everything else, so what's one more thing?" China teased.

"I think we should talk to . . ."

"Daddy."

"No, Magda."

"Why would I hate you for that?"

"Because she'll tell us to talk to Dad."

"Can we just wait one more day? Wait until the campers are gone?"

Deedee nodded. "Maybe we'll have a better idea then."

Reluctantly, the girls returned to camp, deposited Bologna with a sullen Rick, ate lunch, then hung out at the boat shack. The best part was when the lifeguards pestered the lifeguardettes mercilessly as they leaned on the shack, waiting for the campers to come use the lake.

"We *know* you guys did it," Eagle said to Water Lily.

"Did *what?*"

The lifeguards looked at each other. "You can't fool us by playing dumb."

"We are dumb," Katrina said.

"Speak for yourself," Water Lily replied. "We really don't know what you're talking about."

"The sudden flood that came upon us," Richard said.

Deedee hung her head out the window. "What are you guys talking about? I heard someone say something about a flood . . . but there wasn't any rain last night."

Richard's thumb jerked out and pointed at the lifeguardettes. "These young ladies decided to flood our cabin last night."

"That's too bad," China said. "I hope nothing was ruined."

Eagle straightened to his full 6′4″ height. "A bunch of stuff got wet."

"So it will all dry," Deedee offered. Then she smiled sweetly. "I'm sure your friends meant no harm. Just fun."

"We didn't do it," protested Water Lily.

Eagle smiled at her. "Don't worry. We'll make sure you have fun back."

China winked at Deedee.

All afternoon in the kitchen, China's brain worked on finding a solution for Bologna. Her brain, being the dominant monster that it was, wouldn't let her think on anything serious for too long. The thought of losing the dog permanently was so unacceptable that she found herself coming up with new practical jokes, trying to figure out how to transfer old ones, and then would pop in ideas about the dog that were totally nuts.

We could keep him under Deedee's bed. We could tell her dad that he's not a dog, he's a deformed sheep. Deedee and I could move into the old maintenance shack permanently.

"Brain," she said to herself, "you are no help whatsoever."

"Who are you talking to?" John asked, startling her.

"Myself."

"How's Magda?"

"Better."

"Rick told me she was going to be sick for awhile," John said.

"How would he know?" China asked pointedly.

John shrugged. "He goes to see her every day. I guess he just figures by how bad she looks."

Rick's voice sang loudly over the hum of the mixer that chugged away mixing bread dough. "Nothing you can do can make me be untrue to my God, my God . . ."

"Is there a song he doesn't know?" China asked, shaking her head.

"Not that I know of," John said with a smile. "He's so

good at what he does, isn't he? I hope I can run a kitchen like he does one day."

China tilted her head, spatula poised over the Jell-o she was to chop into chunks.

"I think he should be in charge of one of the kitchens at camp, don't you? I'm going to recommend to Mr. Kiersey that he looks into appointing Rick as kitchen manager."

China had trouble listening to him. Her poor brain now had more information it needed to munch on, break down into tiny pieces, and digest. *How would Rick know Magda was going to be sick for awhile?*

Something John said filtered through the jumble. Her head popped up and she looked at John. "Rick as kitchen manager instead of Magda?"

John shrugged. "If she doesn't come back . . ." His voice trailed off as he opened the walk-in door and moved the cart forward at full speed, like always. China heard a loud crack, then something fell to the floor.

John ran around the cart and squatted in front of it. "Oh, man!" He stood, holding the broken security handle in his hand. "Don't tell Rick, okay? I'll get it fixed tomorrow after the campers leave."

"Won't Rick notice?"

"I'll make sure I do all the walk-in work. He's so busy anyway."

China looked at the situation, wondering if she should say anything. At that moment the screen door swung open. "China," Deedee said, her face full of worry. "I need you to take your break right now. Can you?"

John looked at the broken handle in his hand, then at China. "I'll cover for you," he said. China knew what he meant. He'd cover for her if she covered for him. She nodded and ran out the door.

CHAPTER TWELVE

"**W**HAT'S WRONG?" CHINA ASKED as the door closed behind them.

"Magda."

The girls ran to Magda's cabin, not bothering to knock before going in.

Magda moaned and writhed on the bed. "Land sakes, girls," she said, her voice little puffs of air between moans. "This is worse than before."

"Did you eat something?" China asked.

Deedee nodded. "She ate the lunch. Just as she suspected, within three hours it hit her."

"Like always," Magda moaned.

"What do we do now?" China asked, her eyes filling with tears.

"Magda doesn't eat any more special food. I'm going to start bringing simple food from home. Applesauce. Toast," Deedee said firmly.

"What do I do?" China asked, her heart pounding.

"Nothing," Deedee said.

"Nothing!" China almost shouted. "I can't stand around and do nothing."

A plump hand reached toward her from underneath the pale lavender sheet. China took it. "You are where you need to be. You aren't doing nothing," Magda said weakly. "You are my eyes and ears."

And then China remembered what she had heard. She told Magda and Deedee. Tears came to Magda's eyes. "Just listen and tell me what you hear. Okay, China honey? Don't go running to your own conclusions."

When China left, she felt as if her mind would explode. There was too much to keep track of. Too much that hurt. So when Rick grabbed her and put her in dance position, trying to teach her how to cha-cha, she could only laugh and bury all the confusion and wonder about how this total nut case could do anything to hurt anyone. She stepped back when she should have stepped forward. She cha-cha'd when she should have stepped, she moved her shoulders far too much, and in general, had a hilarious time. Bologna danced with them, getting under their feet and loving every minute of it. John clapped the rhythm faster and faster, then threw a towel at them and stomped off.

"What's his problem?" China asked.

"He's jealous."

"Of what?"

"That I have the prettiest girl in camp dancing with

me, working with me, and sharing a dog with me."

China backed up, feeling suddenly awkward. She said the first thing that came into her head. "Whoa! It sounds like we're almost married."

Rick rubbed his chin, pretending to look thoughtful. "Hmmm. Maybe that's a good idea."

China's eyes popped.

Rick smiled a goofy grin. "I'm kidding, you silly. I'm *kidding.*"

"Are not," Carolyn said as she whisked by. "You don't dance with me."

Rick spun around, took her up in perfect dance position, and began to waltz around the kitchen. "Yes I do!"

Carolyn tilted her head back, a throaty laugh bubbling out.

Bologna demanded some attention, so Rick brought out a small bowl of uncut spaghetti. They all laughed as Bologna stuck his nose in the bowl, then backed up, pulling a long strand with him.

When everyone had to get back to work, China's mind chose to contemplate the fun she and Deedee would have when God turned the lights out that night.

The lights didn't go out soon enough for either of them. After dark they still had to wait. Earlier in the day they had tried out their simple sound machine on Deedee's brothers, who loved it. "Cool enough!" Adam had said, itching to get his hands on it.

Joseph smiled and nodded.

"Yeah," Deedee said graciously, "you guys can have it when we're done."

"Who ya gonna scare?" Adam asked, barely able to stand still.

China put her finger to her lips. "It's a secret; we can't tell. But we want you to walk around the beach several times this afternoon and talk about the bear sightings."

"We haven't had any in a couple of weeks," Adam protested.

"Well, talk about them anyway. Just don't say when they happened."

The boys spread the news a couple of times, but then got bored and refused to do it again unless they got paid or were in on the joke.

Now the girls tried to make the time go faster by repeating the strategy again and again to make certain they had it right. But the strategy was simple and there wasn't much to go over.

Finally, it was 9:30. China carried the empty can that had once held enough peaches to serve an army, or two tables of hungry teenage boys. She had cleaned it, poked a hole in the bottom, and put a shoestring through the hole, knotting the end inside the can. Then she wet the shoestring.

Deedee held the plastic pail of water balloons, filled and ready for attack. The green, blue, yellow, and red globes shone slippery and bright in the cabin lights as they passed.

Halfway there, Deedee stopped. "My arm is killing me." She held out the bucket to China and said in a Tarzan voice. "You take it, big, strong Amazon Woman."

China handed her the can. "Watch it, girl, or you might find your mouth full of water balloon."

There were three female lifeguards. The girls watched and counted as they passed the lighted window. "There's an extra," Deedee said with delight. "I wonder who it is."

"Who cares?" China said. "Let's just get 'em."

They positioned themselves to one side of the front door, hidden by the trees, able to run quickly into the forest once they finished their task.

China held the can under her arm, wetting the string one more time. She held onto it with her thumb and forefinger close to the can. As she pulled, her fingers slipped down the string and the can moaned, sounding somewhat like a bear scavenging for food. The bear moaned again. And again. Activity in the cabin picked up. Squeals of girls' voices started to filter through the window.

"They aren't as brave as the guys, are they?" said China.

"Do it again."

China pulled the string and an extra loud moan came.

A loud voice from inside the cabin said, "This is stupid. Get your camera and let's take a picture. He can't get us in here."

The door opened a crack. "I can't see anything."

China pulled the string softly to make the "bear" sound quieter, not so frightening.

The lifeguardettes opened the door all the way and tiptoed out. Three of the four were barefoot. China smiled. *They can't chase us far in bare feet.*

"Now!" China hissed.

They each grabbed two balloons and heaved them at the figures standing in the doorway. Deedee's missed and splattered inside the cabin. China hit one girl in the arm, and another's knees. They grabbed more balloons and heaved them as fast as they could.

In a Three Stooges move, one of the figures tried to slam the door shut, but only succeeded in pinning one person between the door and the jam. Two others were stuck outside in the volley of balloons. As the four tried to get inside, they tripped over the cement pad in front of the cabin and ran into the closing door and each other. Deedee and China threw the can in the empty bucket and ran, desperately trying to hold their laughter until they were out of earshot.

When they knew they were safe, China turned to Deedee. "When are you going to tell them it was you?"

Deedee smiled a mischievous grin. "Probably never."

Saturday morning Deedee reported the sad news to China. "I have to go see my cousins today. My aunt is totally neurotic and only invites two of us kids over at a time. I took a friend once and she threw a fit. She has this thing about family and says it's totally rude for me to bring a friend when I come to see her precious darlings."

"Do you have to go?"

"Mom likes to keep the peace with this aunt."

China stretched out on her sleeping bag bed. "Fine. Ditch me. See if I care."

"China," Deedee pleaded.

"Just kidding, Deeds. I would actually rather stay here than visit people I don't know. I'll do the usual . . . check on Magda, play with Bologna. Maybe I'll even write my mom a letter."

"That'd be a first."

"I know. I wonder if she thinks I fell off a cliff or something."

Deedee opened each drawer of her dresser, rummaged through, and slammed each one closed again. "Uhhhh!" she grunted in frustration. "I hate going to Aunt Elizabeth's house! She's so critical of my clothes."

"So wear mine," China said deviously.

"Funny."

"Seriously. Won't she like missionary barrel clothes? They're so conservative that even a 90-year-old grandmother would approve."

Deedee raised her eyebrows. "True!"

"You can borrow any of my lovely, marvelous possessions . . ."

"Yes?"

"If I can wear something of yours. It's so hot out

there, I think I'll die if I have to wear jeans even one more minute."

Deedee put on a pair of China's long jean shorts, and a baggy lavender T-shirt. "How do I look?"

"Perfectly boring and plain."

"Terrif!"

"Now if you could just lose the hiking boots," China said.

"Aunt Elizabeth would think I'm an imposter. She wouldn't recognize me."

China discovered a pair of Deedee's gold cotton athletic shorts with a faded blue, tie-dye tank top.

Deedee wrinkled her nose. "You clash."

"So? Who's going to see me? A dog, a few trees, and Magda. None of them care, so why should I? I'm going for comfort, not fashion."

"You can say that again."

Deedee's mother apologized profusely for her sister-in-law's quirks, loaded the kids in the van, made sure China would be okay, then left in a cloud of dust.

China stopped by to see Magda, then made her way to the kitchen.

"Where's your other half?" Rick said as she walked in.

"Gone for the day."

"And didn't take you with her?"

"I guess she has a strange aunt who won't let her friends come with her."

"She must have heard about you," Rick teased.

"Must have," China agreed.

"What brings you here?" Rick asked, while he wiped down the prep table. John stood behind him, stirring something on the stove. "It's your day off. You're supposed to be out being young and lazy."

"I intend to be just that. But I had to come by for two reasons. First, I want to get Bologna for the day."

Rick tugged on his blue Dodgers cap. "I counted on you coming. I made other plans that didn't include dog-sitting." He winked at her.

"Am I that predictable?"

"When it comes to the special man, uh, dog in your life, yeah."

China shook her head, her tawny hair covering her blushing face.

"Second reason, please," Rick said.

China crouched to play with Bologna and to wait until her face stopped heating up. "Magda sent me to tell you she won't need lunch. She's not feeling well enough to eat."

John turned from the soup he stirred on the stove. In his hand he held a container of what China assumed was some type of spice. He fastened the bright green lid while he talked to her. "Oh, no! That's too bad. Have you told her I've made my famous chicken soup?"

"I didn't know you cooked," China said, standing back up.

John gave a sweeping bow. "Up and coming five-star chef, at your service."

"Wow. I wish she could eat it, but she's really feeling awful. You can go offer her the soup if you want. I can't go once I have Bologna."

"Okay," he said cheerfully. "I'll do that." China could tell John was trying to keep some emotion from showing on his face, but she couldn't quite get it. His eyes were as unrevealing as always.

"China," Rick said. "I really think Magda should eat."

"I think she's old enough to decide for herself," China teased. "Who made you her father?"

It was Rick's turn to blush, and he turned away.

John turned the heat off underneath the pot of simmering soup. He untied his apron and started for the laundry hamper. "Well, I guess it's about time to start our day off, isn't it, Boss?"

Rick checked his watch. "Just about. We need to make one last sweep of the dining room and kitchen before we go."

"Can we do it fast?" John asked. "I'm really anxious to get started." He looked at China. "With only a little more than 24 hours between campers, every minute counts." John saluted, then went into the dining room.

Rick bent down to scratch Bologna, who wagged his tail as he looked up at his part-time master. "Why don't you get some bologna to take with you for snacks?" Rick suggested to China.

"Thanks."

"There's also some of those peanut butter cookies stashed somewhere in there," Rick offered. "I think you really liked those, didn't you?"

China felt her eyes light up. "Thanks!"

China and Bologna went into the walk-in. She found the lunch meat at the back of the walk-in, directly underneath the blowing fans on a tall cart. Rick and John always made certain the good leftovers were kept on this cart. China pulled the trays out, one at a time, looking for the container of cookies.

Suddenly she felt an eerie sensation, as if someone was looking at her. She turned slowly, just in time to see the door close.

China sighed. She looked at the dog. "I've done it again, Bologna." He wagged his tail, even though he couldn't hear his mistress. She smiled at how he seemed to know everything she said anyway.

"Sorry!" she called lamely toward the closed door.

She should have known the cookies would be on the bottom tray in the very back. Rick hoarded his spare cookies like a miser.

She stacked three in her hand and closed the bag. A faint metallic scratching noise sounded on the other side of the door. She didn't think much of it as she replaced the tray. But as she turned to leave, the light went out in the walk-in.

She froze, scrunching her eyes tight. The old fears prickled the back of her neck. *I am not going to panic, I am not going to panic,* she told herself quietly.

"Yoohoo!" she called. "Turn on the light, please."

She edged her way forward, trying to picture the crates and cans on the floor. *Did she walk around any on her way in?* She put her right hand on a shelf, using it as a guide. Bologna bounced around her ankles, encouraging her to move ahead. "I can't see, Bologna."

She'd seen movies of people who were blind. Even watched an old, blind Mayan Indian woman move about the market. They shuffled their feet like China did now, slowly, so there would be no surprises to bump or trip them. Items that were obvious in the light became confusing lumps in the dark.

Relief flooded her when she reached the door, even though it felt cold, hard, and unyielding beneath her hand. She slid her hand over the surface, trying to find the handle.

The handle! Her hand moved frantically now, searching for the handle she had forgotten wasn't there. It was broken off. Gone. She and John had made a pact. A silent one. And Rick didn't know. He hardly ever went into the walk-in himself. If Rick had closed the door to save energy, he wouldn't know she couldn't get out. "Rick?" she called. "Rick!"

But what if he didn't know she was in there? What if he thought she had left? He would have padlocked the door and turned out the light. He wouldn't return for over 24 hours! "RICK! JOHN!" she called, pounding on the door. But no matter how hard she hit the door, it barely made a muffled whump on her side. Surely no one could hear it on the other side.

Just as she raised her hand to strike the door again, she remembered, *Rick locks the walk-in as the last thing he does before he leaves. He never, ever does anything else first.*

China leaned her head against the door, her heart pounding inside her chest. *I'm stuck. Trapped. There's no way out.*

CHAPTER THIRTEEN

OKAY, OKAY, CALM DOWN. THINK. The broken
door handle had to have left a hole in the door. Or a
piece of plastic in the hole. It was a simple handle,
anyway. Pretty much like a large knob on the end of
a stick. The stick end was about as big around as her
finger. Her hands fluttered over the door, finding the
edge, then moving downward to find where the handle had been. It took some time, as the handle had
not been near the edge of the door at all, but a number of inches toward the center of it.

China's fingers found the spot. The handle had
broken off just inside the hole, leaving a rough, un-
even edge behind. China poked at it with her finger,
glad she had never bothered with fancy nails like
Heather's. Pushing at the remaining plastic nub didn't
do a thing. Her finger bent oddly at the first knuckle
and didn't have the right pressure to push the plastic.
If the plastic had been smooth, it might have helped
somewhat. But one edge ridged closer to the hole

than the rest, making the hole too small for her finger, and the plastic difficult to push.

Every few minutes she shivered and rubbed her arms for warmth. Bologna sat next to her left ankle, giving her leg a reassuring lick each time she rubbed her arms. Her finger was sore from trying so hard to open the door. She decided to give it a rest and turned her back to the door, sliding to the ground. Bologna made the most of the moment by hopping onto her lap, reaching up to furiously lick her face.

"Thank you, Bologna, that's enough. Thank you. Good dog." China put her hand firmly on his back, encouraging him to sit down. Bologna curled in her lap and rested his head on her knee.

Her breathing sounded funny. Choppy. Heavy. *Like I'm scared out of my mind. Stop it!*

China's hand automatically began to stroke the soft head in her lap. She placed her other hand on the floor for support. Instead of feeling cold cement as she expected, she felt a rumpled piece of paper. "It feels like a label," she said to Bologna who didn't move.

It felt like a label on one side, but on the other it seemed to have little pieces of something stuck to it. She held it up in front of her face turning it over and over. She couldn't see a thing.

Her lips felt funny and dry in the cold.

"We've got to get away from these fans," China told Bologna. She put him on the floor, then got on all fours herself. With each crawling step, her hands swept over the floor and under the shelves. *Which shelf is highest off the ground?* China measured, her hand raising from the floor to the bottom of the iron shelf. Several times she raised it too fast, whacking her hand on the freezing metal.

With each minute that passed, it felt as though some huge mouth bit into her bones.

Sit still! China ordered herself. *Sit still and think. What does the walk-in look like?*

Dark. Narrow. Like a box.

She shivered. *NO! Not like a box. Like a hallway. Like a place that has more than one way to get out.*

How do you tell yourself not to be scared? How do you convince yourself that there is nothing to be afraid of when there's everything to be afraid of?

The cold covered her skin, an unwelcome blanket coating it with a layer of prickles. *Can you freeze to death in a 40-degree refrigerator?*

The question is, can you find a way to keep warmer in a long, cold hallway?

China again pictured the walk-in. Which shelves were high off the floor. Where the crates sat stacked against a wall. Where the tall carts waited with layers of trays.

To the left. Near the back. Near the cold air fans.

China crawled forward, making mental note of the things she encountered. A crate of milk. Butter. Produce. Lunch meats. Huge containers of condiments. Jugs of syrup. Quarts of yogurt.

At least I won't starve, she thought with a small smile.

The shelves near the back had a space large enough for her to crawl underneath the wire racks. She flattened her belly to the ground and scooted to the wall, curling into a small ball to keep warm. But cold air from the fans circulated around her—a very cold cocoon.

Pushing Bologna out first, she crawled back out and began moving things. All the crates she could find she stacked around her cubbyhole. She put tall carts behind those. Reaching underneath another set of shelves, she dragged out a heavy crate filled with something she couldn't discern. As she pulled it away from the wall a red glow filled the spot like a gaping wound.

Little aliens, her sluggish mind offered.

China lay on her belly to check it out. An electrical outlet with a tiny red light poking out of the cover plate glowed steadily in the darkness. China stared at it as if it were a dear friend. Bologna lay next to her, watching to see what was so interesting about this red light.

The cold air blew on China's legs, waking her to the need to get out of the chill. As she moved, the mysterious paper crinkled in her shorts pocket. Her hand, feeling fat and numb, pulled it out. One side told her it was from a pickle jar. The other had letters pasted to it.

China rolled her eyes. "Oh, brother. Can you believe this, Bologna? Someone is trying to play murder mystery or something. How stupid; can't they be more original?"

Like a kid's building blocks tumbled on the floor, the letters scattered on the page.

S C A R E D ?

G O O D

She stared at the words. She read them once, twice, five times. She understood the words. Why wouldn't she? They were simple. They were probably on her brother Nic's third-grade spelling word list.

But she didn't understand what they meant. Who would do that? Why? Were they meant for her?

The cold took bites out of her flesh. Nips and gulps. She lay the note down and crawled back to her cubby. Once inside, she couldn't feel the wind of the fans as much. Bologna joined her, curling up close to her belly. His body made a spot of warmth against her.

All her insides quivered with fear. The outside shivered with cold. Each breath brought the cold inside her body. *Cover your mouth **and** nose.* She pulled the tank top up enough to cover her nose and breathe through the fabric. Her mind twirled and tossed horrifying thoughts into the air. She tried to shut it down, but it screamed louder at her.

Someone planned for you to be locked in this place.

Who?

Rick?

She remembered Rick's anger at her. His insistence that the walk-in door stay shut at all times. *He closed the door on you once before. He knew you were scared. He said you were cute when you were scared.*

Warm tears trickled down China's cold face, sliding off into her ear. "Why would someone hate me so much?" she asked Bologna.

John? Unpredictable John?

Nothing was good enough for John.

But he wasn't in the kitchen. Rick told you to go in the walk-in.

Were they in on it together? Were both doing something to Magda's food to make her sick?

Over and over, China thought about every detail she could remember of the past week. Nothing gave her a definite answer. Rick played jokes on her. But would he think this was a funny joke?

The thought of the two guys purposefully locking her in the cold, dark place hurt all the way down to the core of her. Heather's hatred was child's play compared to this.

God, I'm so, so scared. I'm so cold it hurts. Can you please help me get through this? No one will even know I'm missing until late tonight. I could be dead by then.

China prayed for everyone she knew. Her parents, Aunt Liddy, her brothers, the kids at the missionary school in Guatemala. Deedee's family, Magda, Kemper, the whole camp, even Heather, until exhaustion, fueled by fear, took her to sleep.

Somewhere, a blizzard raged. She could hear the wind blowing, blowing. Heavy. Numb. Three-hundred-pound weights pushed her body into the hard ground of the dark cave. Her slow breathing barely lifted her chest. Something wet traveled across her cheek. She lifted a fat arm. Fat fingers on the end of the fat arm reached to touch the wet thing. Furry wet thing. Dog muzzle.

Opening heavy-lidded eyes didn't help. No light came in except a faint red glow from somewhere far away. The dog's tongue moved all over her face. Frantic licks. Then yelps. Pleas for something. *For what?*

Moving the heavy body took more energy than it was worth the effort. She lay back down, wanting to sleep.

The dog yapped and barked and yipped and licked. "Go away," a husky voice said. "Leave me alone." The barks brought her mind up higher, a mountain peak nosing through the fog.

An uncomfortable, persistent pleading alerted her brain, begging for relief.

Between the dog and the pleading, she had to get up. She tried to sit, her head knocking something above it. She felt the wire shelving, laid back down, and did a marine crawl to the outside where the wind blew. In her fumblings, she found a half-full can of pears and emptied it onto the floor. Bologna lapped eagerly at the sticky liquid. Humiliating tears streamed down her face as she pulled down her shorts and sat on the can. The relief of one discomfort made her intensely aware of another.

Liquid lead shifted in the pit of her stomach. *Am I hungry? Or will I throw up?*

She gave Bologna lunch meat. This time he didn't dance. Her own stomach rejected the cookies she offered it. She abandoned them to the dog and searched the walk-in for yogurt. She opened the lids and smelled. The peach smell added another twist to her hurting heart and flipped her upset stomach. She dipped two fingers into the strawberry. Licking them clean, she dipped again. After a few dips, her stomach lurched again. She closed the lid and inched back to her cave.

Bologna barked sharply at her and ran toward the door, then back to her, then to the door again.

"You want out of here?" China asked, her voice raw and husky. "Me too. But there's no way out."

Try.

It wasn't her fogged brain talking. It was something else.

Find something for the hole.

China moved about the walk-in, feeling everything within reach. She found a table knife, a rubber spatula, tin foil, a bent serving spoon and a mustard dispenser. The knife, the spoon, and the spatula were all too big to fit in the hole. The cone tip of the mustard dispenser fit in the hole, but not deep enough to push the plastic. She rolled the tin foil into a rod-shape, but it lacked the strength to push hard enough.

China leaned her weary head against the door. "I give up."

No, you don't. Try again.

She stuck her finger in the hole, wishing she could somehow dismantle one of the shelves, using the metal rod to gain freedom. She grabbed the closest shelf, shaking it with fury and determination. Cans toppled and rolled on the floor, hitting Bologna. A sharp yelp stopped China in her tracks. She knelt down, waiting for Bologna to come to her. "I'm so sorry, boy. I'm sorry," she said, cuddling him close.

Setting him on the floor, she moved to the hinged side of the door and felt along the shelves, but they too were welded together.

On the top shelf, her hands discovered a clipboard. She quickly felt the clip, and sure enough, a pen hid underneath it. Shoving the pen in the hole, her numb hands slipped, unable to grasp the pen tightly enough.

She wrapped the pen with the bottom of her tank top and jammed it in the hole as hard as she could. Her eyes immediately swam with tears of pain. She jammed it again and again, but she couldn't get enough pressure behind the pen. The cold had left her too weak.

Taking a large, unopened can of fruit from the

shelf, she again placed the pen in the hole, the can against the pen. *Dear God, get me out of here!* As she prayed, she leaned her whole weight against the can.

CHAPTER FOURTEEN

THE DOOR SWUNG OPEN into a dark kitchen. Dark yet light. Light compared to total darkness. Dark, empty, and lonely. Without dancing. Without music, singing, work, and play. Dark with pain.

Bologna wandered out, his tilt increased. His tail wagged slowly as he checked out the room. China took a pan from the rack above her head. She staggered to the sink and turned on the hot water. When it felt warm to her cold hands, she filled the pan and put it in front of Bologna. His pink tongue lapped once, as if tasting water for the first time. Then it lapped faster, darting in and out quickly.

China kept her wrists under the running water, adding cold water to keep the temperature from getting too hot. As the warm water ran over her wrists, she could feel the warmth ooze into her blood stream and begin to spread with needling pain into the rest of her body.

What time was it? Had anyone missed her?

151

More than anything, China wanted to go to sleep. She felt sick to her stomach.

The odor of soup turned her head. The pot sat there, still full. Next to the pot, on the counter, a tall container with a bright green lid stood guard.

China turned off the water and wiped her hands on a nearby towel. She picked up the container and stared at the label. Monosodium Glutamate (MSG). The other side told her it was a natural flavoring to enhance a food's own flavor. She shrugged her shoulders and set it back down.

China turned to leave and saw the walk-in door ajar. She trembled as she stepped closer to shut it. Inside were pears half-eaten by Bologna. Crates and carts moved. The can of humiliation.

I can't leave that.

Opening the door as wide as it would go, she propped it open with a heavy pot. With pen in hand, just in case, she ventured back into the cold prison. Bologna yapped furiously. China picked up the can and ran out, her heart pounding in her chest. She poured the contents down the soaking sink and poured half a jug of blue liquid silverware sterilizer after it. Then she put the can into the high-powered, sterilizing dishwasher. Two minutes later the cycle was done. Gingerly she picked up the hot metal can and dropped it into the garbage can.

"Let's get out of here, Bologna." She wiggled her fingers at the little black dog.

As she passed the stove, something clicked in her brain. She picked up the container of MSG and left the kitchen.

Walking somewhat like Bologna, she moved her heavy feet one at a time in the direction of Magda's cabin. The sun hung low in the sky. Bologna watered every bush and tree in sight.

Without knocking, China walked into Magda's cabin, Bologna at her heels.

"Why China honey!" Magda said, putting her book down in her lap. "And a dog?!" A moment later, she stood, her book falling from her lap. "Oh my, whatever is wrong?"

China walked over to Magda's bed and flopped on it. Bologna leapt up beside her and curled protectively against her belly.

"China honey, where have you been?" Her loving hands rested on China's leg.

"The walk-in."

"What?"

"The walk-in. Since Rick closed up."

"That was seven hours ago!"

"Oh," China replied, uncaring.

"Why didn't you let yourself out?"

"The handle broke. Yesterday."

"Didn't they know you were in there?"

China put a shaky hand into her pocket, withdrawing the pickle label. "I found this."

Magda read it, then set it on the table. "Oh, dear.

Oh, dear." She began to pace, her hand pushing away tendrils of hair that weren't there.

China held out the container of MSG. "What's this?"

Magda stopped her pacing. She took the container from China and read it. "Where'd you get this?"

"The kitchen."

"I stopped using this years ago."

"Is it bad?"

"Only for some people. Most people eat MSG all the time and don't even notice. It's a common additive to make food taste better. But for those of us who are allergic to it, it can cause us to be terribly ill." Magda stopped. She grabbed a chair and plopped in it. "I hadn't had MSG in so long, I'd forgotten."

"John was putting it in the soup he was making you for lunch yesterday."

"John?" Magda took China's hands in hers. She looked right through China, staring at her, but not seeing. "Did Rick know?"

China shrugged. "I guess."

China could almost see gears turning. Magda's loving eyes seemed to grow darker with sadness. A tear trickled down Magda's cheek. "My boys," she whispered. "My poor boys."

China closed her eyes, feeling so tired. "I'm sorry, Magda," she said. "I just want to sleep."

Magda leaned forward, caressing China's hair. "Before you sleep, introduce me to the dog. I assume this is the hungry, thirsty creature you found?"

China nodded. "Bologna."

"Bologna?"

China's voice came soft and wispy. "The dog's name is Bologna. He's deaf."

When she awoke, lights were on in the cabin. Deedee sat by the bed, holding Bologna. Magda sat her overstuffed body in the overstuffed chair. Mr. Kiersey sat on the sofa. The two spoke in quiet voices.

"Hey, you," Deedee said. "How're you doing, Frog?"

China smiled. "I'm warm, I'm awake. I'm fine, Toad." She lifted herself on one elbow. "How was Aunt Elizabeth?"

"As strange as ever. At least she liked my clothes." Deedee looked over at her father and Magda. "So what's the deal? What happened?"

China lost her smile. "I don't know." She shuddered. "I don't want to think about it."

"I hate to say this," Deedee said, looking at her dad. "But I'm glad my dad's here. I think he'll find out what happened."

"I'm glad he's here, too," China said. "I guess sometimes I can't do it all myself."

Deedee told China stories about Aunt Elizabeth while Mr. Kiersey talked at length with Magda. Then he came and took Deedee's seat.

"You've had a rough time at camp, China. If you decide you want to go home, we can arrange that."

Last week China would have thought he wanted her to go. This week she could read the sadness etching his face. "I don't want to go," China said. "But I sure seem to cause a lot of trouble."

"I think you are simply a person who has strong values. And you don't let others push those values into their mold. They don't like that, and they fight back."

China swallowed. She didn't know if she'd ever had such a compliment. She didn't know what to do with it.

"People like you tend to show others their own guilt."

"But I haven't pointed an accusing finger at anyone," China protested.

"You don't have to. Working hard, respecting those in authority, refusing to be manipulated or put someone above you who doesn't belong there . . . these are things that make other people mad." Mr. Kiersey sighed, pushing his fingertips together. "Mad enough to lock you in the walk-in."

China looked down at the bed, picking at a thread that stuck out of the quilt.

"Do you know who did it?" Mr. Kiersey asked.

China shook her head. "I've thought a lot about it, but I can't decide if it was an accident or on purpose."

"The note tells me it was on purpose. Why don't you fill me in on what happened when you went into the kitchen."

China thought a moment. "I think I really should begin with the first day of the week."

Mr. Kiersey nodded.

China began with the moment she met Rick and continued to when she let herself out of the walk-in, stopping only to take sips on the grape juice Magda offered. Mr. Kiersey nodded, pushed his fingertips together, and occasionally asked a clarifying question. When China finished, Mr. Kiersey stood. "Do you mind if the girls stay with you, Magda?"

"Of course not."

Mr. Kiersey turned to walk out the door. He tapped his daughter on the nose. "We'll discuss the dog later, young lady."

When the door closed behind him, Magda turned, hands on her hips to face the girls. "What have you girls been up to behind my back?"

China sat up on the bed, her back against the wall, pillow in her lap. Deedee joined her, the dog draped across her knees.

They looked at each other.

"Well?" Magda said.

"You first," China said, poking Deedee. "I've already been spilling my guts."

"You found him."

"Deedee," Magda said firmly. "Speak."

"Woof?" Deedee said. China giggled.

Magda tried to look stern, but a smile played at the corners of her mouth.

"Okay, okay," Deedee said. Another story, details added by China, filled the tiny cabin.

At first Magda sat with her arms crossed. When she

heard about the people who thought Bologna should be put to sleep because he was deaf, she dropped her arms and shook her head. The girls left out the part about throwing food on the ceiling in the kitchen, although they did confess Bologna had spent most of his present life in her hallowed halls of cooking.

"If there is ONE dog hair . . ." Magda interrupted.

"He doesn't shed," Deedee said lamely. "So we thought it might be okay. For a short while."

Magda tried to look mean and angry. But it didn't work. "He can't stay there no more."

"We know," China said. "We've been trying to think of where he could go. But we haven't figured it out yet."

The cabin shook as someone pounded on the door.

"Come in!" Magda called.

The door opened and Rick stood there, arms dangling loosely at his sides. He glanced quickly about the cabin, stopping when he saw China. "Are you okay?" His long legs covered the distance quickly.

No one said anything. China felt a new shiver run up her back. She looked down at her hands.

"I just heard. Mr. Kiersey told me. I didn't know. I feel so awful."

China looked at him again. *Did he really not know? Did he really feel awful?*

"Why, Rick?" Magda said softly. "Why do you feel so bad?" Her hands trembled in her lap.

Rick looked at the three of them. "You think I did this? You think I did this on purpose?" He lifted his

Dodgers cap and ran his fingers through his hair. He walked toward the sitting area and plopped on the sofa, his head in his hands. "Magda, you know me. You know who I am."

"I also know how many times people have looked at that curled hand and limp and have decided you couldn't be worth much. How many girlfriends have you had? Any girls willing to find the treasure I know is buried inside that imperfect body?"

China bit her lip, ashamed that she could hardly see him as even a friend for that very reason.

Rick looked down at his hand, inspecting it. "Girls don't give me a chance. China and Deedee are the first to really treat me like maybe I might be okay."

Relief filled China. At least he hadn't noticed her hesitance. *I vow to give you a chance, Rick Marshall. You are fun. I think.*

"That has to hurt, Rick. And what about Matt's death? That hurt you more than I've seen death hurt anyone before. You loved him with all your gentle, genuine, soft heart. But you couldn't let anyone know how much you cared. Or they'd slap one of them ugly labels on you."

"Who's Matt?" China whispered to Deedee.

Deedee's eyebrows raised, her uplifted hands saying, "I don't know."

"So what has that got to do with this, Magda?"

"People with big hurts sometimes do things to hurt others."

Rick leaned forward, his forearms resting on his knees. He twirled his Dodger cap around in his hands, looking to it as if it might have the answers he needed. "Yeah, I loved him. But I learned from him the things you taught him. I wouldn't hurt anyone on purpose."

"What about when you grabbed my wrists and told me I owed you one?" China blurted out.

Rick's jaw dropped. "Did I hurt you?" He looked down at his hat. "I was just trying to make you laugh. Like one of the movies where the guy does something . . . oh, forget it. I'm sorry, China. Really. I didn't mean to hurt you."

China looked at the person on the couch. It was the body of a man, looking oddly like that of a child. "I believe you," she said finally.

Rick nodded, then continued talking to Magda. "Ever since Matt died in a horrible car accident, I started watching musicals like he did. Every time I sing a song, every time I find a place where a song from a musical applies, it's like Matt is still here. Like I can go on without his friendship."

Rick dropped his hat on the sofa, walked over to the girls, and sat on the floor next to Magda. Looking at China and Deedee, he said, "I must admit that I've been jealous of your friendship. It hurt to see you guys together. When I saw how you guys were so close and having so much fun, I missed Matt all over again."

"Maybe we can get to know you better as a friend," China said. "I know I'd like that." To her surprise, China realized she meant it. With every ounce of her, she meant it. It didn't matter what he looked like. His heart was worth knowing. This tender, sensitive, fun, sincere heart was more important than anything else. He'd never be a model. He'd never win a prize for his looks. It didn't matter anymore.

Rick smiled softly. "Thanks. That means a lot."

It must have. His jaw tightened and he swallowed hard, breathing deeply.

Deedee broke in. "I'm sorry to interrupt, but who is Matt?"

Rick looked at her, his eyes round and sad. "He was my best friend."

Magda hiccupped a kind of sob. "He was my son."

CHAPTER FIFTEEN

Mɢᴅᴀ'ꜱ ʜᴀɴᴅꜱ ᴄᴏᴠᴇʀᴇᴅ ʜᴇʀ ꜰᴀᴄᴇ. Rick moved to his knees and wrapped his arms around her. For a long time they sat together crying.

China and Deedee could do nothing but look at each other, then back at Magda and Rick.

Finally, Rick swiped at his face, looking embarrassed. "I've known Magda since I was 13 and a real jerk. Matt and I made life miserable for everybody around us."

"But you was both good kids," Magda said, kissing Rick on the top of his head.

"I doubt that," Rick said. "Anyway, Matt pulled out of it sooner than I did, dragging me along with him. He was great at music. Played a wild keyboard. His hobby was musicals. *Sound of Music, My Fair Lady, Music Man*, even stuff like *Mary Poppins, Joseph and His Technicolor Dreamcoat*, and *Phantom of the Opera*."

"Don't forget *Les Misérables*," Magda urged.

Rick sat back on his haunches, a faraway look spreading over his face. "Yeah. It was Les Miz that taught me about God's incredible way of taking an ugly past or an ugly person and making that person's life count for something good. That everyone has value and deserves a chance to be loved."

Rick sat up and looked at China. "That's why you have to believe I wouldn't hurt you." He turned to Magda. "I've changed, Magda. I haven't hurt anybody for a long time."

"Then who locked me in the walk-in? You're always the one who locks up the kitchen."

Rick put his head down. "I feel so awful, China. I really do. I went to do one last round of the dining room doors. When I got back, John had padlocked the walk-in and was waiting for me so we could leave together. I asked him if you had left, and he said yes. I never, ever thought you were still inside."

Magda put her hand on Rick's head. "What about my meals this week? Who cooked them?"

"I did."

"With MSG?"

A cloud of confusion passed over his face. He turned to look at her. "Why would I cook with MSG? You told me it was forbidden. Besides, I thought you were allergic to it."

China snapped her fingers. "Wait a minute. Didn't you tell John to stir stuff when it was cooking?"

"Yeah . . ."

Magda broke in. "How has John been this week?"

"Kinda moody, I guess. One minute he'd be happy and acting crazy with the rest of us. The next, he'd be agitated about something or other."

"Like what?" Magda probed.

"I don't know. He was never real clear about what was bothering him. He talked a lot about a woman's place not being over a man. He doesn't much like you being in charge of the kitchen, Magda."

"And what about China?"

"What about her?"

"What does John think about her?"

"I never thought much about what he said. I figured he rambled on about stupid-jerk kind of things. So I didn't pay much attention. Sometimes it got on my nerves."

"What did he say?" China asked quietly.

"I don't really want to say, China. It's not true, so what does it matter?"

"It matters," Magda said firmly. "Tell us."

"He thought China was spoiled, pampered, and a little too high and mighty for her own good. A couple of times he suggested we hide in the forest and scare her so she'd realize her place as a female needing men to help her do everything, rather than being so independent."

"Go on," Magda said, sounding amused.

"He didn't think any female could do things for herself." A thought lit up his face. "The thing that really made him mad was when China beat him in an arm wrestling match."

"You did *what?*" Magda said, looking at China.

China shrugged. "I'm stronger than I look. It's fun to surprise guys with it."

"I think this time you messed with the wrong guy," Magda said.

Rick's eyes got wide and he sat up straight. "You don't think John locked you in the walk-in on purpose do you? He wouldn't do that. He probably thought he heard the screen door close. No, he wouldn't hurt anyone."

China told him about the note.

Rick hung his head, wringing his hands. "He asked me if he could have an old *Sports Illustrated* of mine. I didn't think anything of it."

Bologna jumped from the bed and stood in front of the cabin door. Pacing back and forth, he began to whine a little.

"I'll take him out," China said. She slid off the bed and took the leash from the table.

"I'll go with you," Deedee said.

"Don't go far," Magda begged.

The cool, pine-scented mountain air swept over the girls as they stepped outside. China lifted her face to the sky to feel the fresh, free glory of it all. Bologna tugging on the end of the leash brought her mind back to the solid present.

"What do you think?" Deedee asked.

"I think I totally misread Rick."

Deedee nodded.

"You can say, 'I told you so' now."

"No," Deedee said, stretching her arms above her head, then bending to touch her toes. "I'm just glad that maybe I'll have my fun friend back."

"What will happen to John, do you think?"

"Dad will probably do what's best for the camp. He has a pretty good record in that department."

"And what will become of Bologna?"

Deedee stopped stretching. "I don't know."

Bologna finished his anointing, and China led him back inside the cabin. Rick and Magda were reminiscing about Matt and about Rick's past, so the girls went back outside to sit on the stoop. Within minutes, Mr. Kiersey came up the walk, a look of disturbed authority on his face. He stopped to look at the girls and motioned them inside.

Rick stood when he saw Mr. Kiersey. He nodded but didn't seem to know what else to do.

"Let's sit in the living room," Mr. Kiersey suggested.

The group found seats on the sofa and floor. Bologna looked at them with wide, disappointed eyes. "He's bored," Deedee whispered to China, who nodded.

Mr. Kiersey confirmed what they already knew. John had locked China in the refrigerator in order to scare her into leaving and to repay her for humiliating him.

"So what happens now?" Magda asked.

"If he had been even the least bit remorseful, I would have placed him in another part of camp. But he acted as though it was appropriate action for the situation. He couldn't understand why I wouldn't fire Magda and China both for their 'inappropriate attitudes' toward men."

China tilted her head. "What is my inappropriate attitude?"

Mr. Kiersey leaned forward and looked at her evenly. "He didn't feel it was right for you to view males as friends or equals in any way."

"Is that wrong?"

"No, China. I see in you the proper respect toward anyone in authority. And being friends with someone of the opposite gender is a prize too many people ignore."

Mr. Kiersey leaned forward and ruffled her hair. His fond look sent a warm fuzzy right into her heart. *I almost feel like I'm another daughter.*

"So what will happen to John, Daddy?"

"I'm sending him to a friend of mine who helps young men change harmful attitudes to a more accurate biblical perspective. He also helps them get jobs where they will not harm anyone until they are ready to go back into the mainstream."

No one said anything for a long time. China felt sad for John but hopeful he would get help. Magda stood and put a kettle on her hotplate, offering tea to everyone.

With a steaming mug in his hands, Mr. Kiersey looked at Bologna, then at Deedee. "Tell me all about it."

Deedee went through the story a second time, emphasizing in detail the two times Bologna had helped China. Mr. Kiersey stared hard at his daughter and said, "I get the picture. You can go on now." He frowned when he heard about the kitchen, asking for more details about that part.

Deedee finished the story, paused, then said, "Can we keep him, please, Dad?"

Rick cleared his throat. "He's really a nice dog, Mr. Kiersey. Pleasant. He needs to learn a few manners. But he can do it. I'm sure it will just take longer since he's deaf."

The girls stared at Rick. They turned to look at each other. China mouthed to Deedee, "He's on our side!" Deedee nodded, then turned to look at her father.

Mr. Kiersey looked around the room at the hopeful faces. "I don't make decisions like this quickly. I'll let you know tomorrow. In the meantime, Bologna can stay with Rick another night."

Deedee's face fell.

"Come, girls. We need to leave Magda. She still isn't well enough for all this. And China needs some rest before the new whirlwind of campers comes in tomorrow."

CHAPTER SIXTEEN

MR. KIERSEY WALKED BETWEEN the two girls, his arm around his daughter as the three moved in silence.

A low moan came from somewhere up the mountainside. Then another. "Bear." Mr. Kiersey stated matter-of-factly.

China turned to look at Deedee, but she didn't move her head at all. A tiny smile played around the corners of her mouth.

"Seems like we've had several more bear sightings lately," he continued. "The rangers told me a couple weeks ago they expect the bears might come into camp soon. We have to keep a look out."

The girls remained silent, heads facing forward.

When they came abreast of the boat shack, Mr. Kiersey spoke again. "Seems some lifeguards had a sighting."

China almost choked.

"Seems this bear came armed with water balloons."

Deedee sputtered.

"Smart bears," he continued. "Seems to me they'd be smarter if they let this kind of fun be reciprocated." He sighed. "But, I guess since bears don't talk, they can't straighten up the misunderstanding between the lifeguards and lifeguardettes that's threatening to cause disharmony this summer."

"Well, we're almost home," he announced. "I'm exhausted from bears, dogs, balloons, complaints, confusions, and trying to sort it all out. See you girls in the morning." He trotted up the steps ahead of them, leaving them to stare after him.

In the Kiersey kitchen, Deedee made a batch of extra butter Pop-Secret microwave popcorn. China sliced two apples and poured iced tea. Sitting at the kitchen table in the quiet house, the girls rehashed the bizarre events of the long day. China wolfed down the food, not realizing how hungry she'd been. Deedee popped another bag of popcorn and poured it into the bowl littered with kernels.

"What do you think your dad will decide to do about Bologna?"

Deedee shook her head, then pulled her long curls away from her face. "Can't tell."

China sighed. "One thing I've learned about your dad . . . he's tough, but he's pretty fair."

Deedee nodded. "Yeah. But I'm still scared."

China's thoughts tried to keep her awake, but for once in her life, the fatigue took over quickly.

The next morning neither girl could sit still in the small mountainside church. Quick glances at Mr. Kiersey didn't reveal his thoughts. The man paid full attention to the pastor, while China had no clue of even one point the Pastor tried to make. She desperately wanted to write notes to Deedee but didn't want to risk any chances of having Bologna stay with them.

After a tense lunch, Mr. Kiersey asked the girls to go for a walk to the creek with him.

"Can I walk, too, Daddy?" Eve begged.

"Walk," Anna repeated, smashing her hot dog pieces into the ketchup puddle on her plate.

"I'll come get you girls after Deedee and China have a turn, okay?"

"Goody!" Eve shouted, clapping her hands and spinning around the room.

"Walk," Anna said, carefully watching a ketchup-covered hot dog chunk leave her fingers and splot! on the clean kitchen floor.

"I don't know why I bother," sighed Deedee's mom.

China and Deedee walked down the front steps of the house, feeling Mr. Kiersey's eyes on their backs. He said nothing until they found rock seats on the banks of Grizzly Creek.

"Funny how dogs can so easily become a part of our lives," he began. "Their crazy expressions." He chuckled, shaking his head. "I remember a dog we had when I was a kid . . . before we knew I was allergic. I could have sworn that mutt smiled when she saw me coming. She could look bewildered, happy, disgusted, sad . . . all with those big brown eyes and dangly ears. I could tell her anything."

China poked Deedee.

He looked at his daughter. "I have always felt awful that you had to suffer because I'm allergic. I never thought it was terribly fair. But, there's no way we can have the dog in the house. And it's dangerous for a little guy like that to be chained outside all the time. So I had to eliminate the idea that you could have him for your very own."

"Daddy . . ." Deedee pleaded.

Mr. Kiersey rubbed his hands on his shorts. "I talked to Rick, and I think we can work something out. That is if you are willing."

Deedee's eyes looked hopeful. China tugged her hair behind her ear.

"Rick can keep the dog at night, just like now, and you girls watch him during the day. I would rather he was in the boat shack with you, Deedee, than in the kitchen with China. I don't want the Health Department closing us up because of a dog, no matter how special he is."

"Okay, Dad. We'll take real good care of him, I promise."

Mr. Kiersey put up a silencing hand. "And you'll pay for half his food. Rick pays for the other half. Rick will take him to the vet first thing Monday morning for shots and a check-up. You girls will pay half of that visit also. Clear?"

Both girls nodded.

"Be careful with him and don't let him get into trouble. I want him trained to sign language as soon as possible." Mr. Kiersey slapped his thighs and stood up. "I'm sorry I must leave you ladies, but I have a date with two little girls."

The girls ran all the way to the kitchen to tell Magda and Rick the good news. They wove in and out of the clutch of new, bewildered campers, then burst into the kitchen, out of breath.

Magda sat on a chair, looking like she'd be better off with one more day of rest before she hit the pots and pans.

"We get to keep him!" they shouted.

"How nice," Magda said, every ripple and wave smiling with her.

"You agreed to share him?" Rick asked.

They nodded.

"Hooray!" Rick said, grabbing China and spinning her around the kitchen. His tenor voice belted out, a song from Mary Poppins telling them all how lucky he was to a squeever.

"What is a squeever, anyway?" China squealed.

Rick stopped dead, China almost falling over with the sudden end to the dance. "I don't know. I guess it's a chimney sweep who draws on the sidewalk."

Rick ran over to Deedee, swept her up and began his wild spin around the kitchen once again. He let

Deedee go, and went to Magda, hand outstretched. Magda looked up at him. "You've lost your mind, boy. Magda don't dance. No waltz. No spins. No polka. None. Zero."

"Too bad," Rick said with a huge pout. "You're missing out on the time of your life."

"Maybe so. But I'd like to live to see tomorrow. These kids gotta eat."

"We got along fine without you for one week. We could do another," he teased.

Magda lifted her wooden spoon, as if to throw it at him. She stopped and looked beyond Rick's head. As she stared at the ceiling, a look of puzzlement settled on her soft features. "What . . . ?"

She squinted her eyes to get a better look. Everyone else looked up too. "Why, it looks like . . ." She walked around staring at the greasy patterns spotting her perfect kitchen ceiling. The guilty parties stared at each other, wondering if they should tell her. Bologna, noticing all their attention focused above, began to dance and bark.

Magda waved a hand at him without looking down. "Shush."

She wandered around a bit more. "It looks like some creature's been walkin' up there! I'd swear them things is footprints."

China stepped forward. "It's bologna, Magda. Bologna on the ceiling."

Magda stood up straighter than China had ever

seen her. "You're pullin' my leg, China honey, and I don't like it."

"No, really," Deedee affirmed. "It really is bologna on the ceiling. It's the marks left behind."

Magda looked at all the faces in front of her, each one nodding in serious affirmation. She looked down at the dog, who danced his jig, looking hopefully upward.

"Well, I'll be," she muttered. "Bologna on the ceiling?" Everyone nodded again. She turned away, shaking her head, muttering to herself. "How'd they get him up there, anyway? Who'da thought a dog could walk on a ceiling?"

Suddenly it dawned on everyone why Magda had been so skeptical. At once, they all fell to the floor, laughing hysterically.

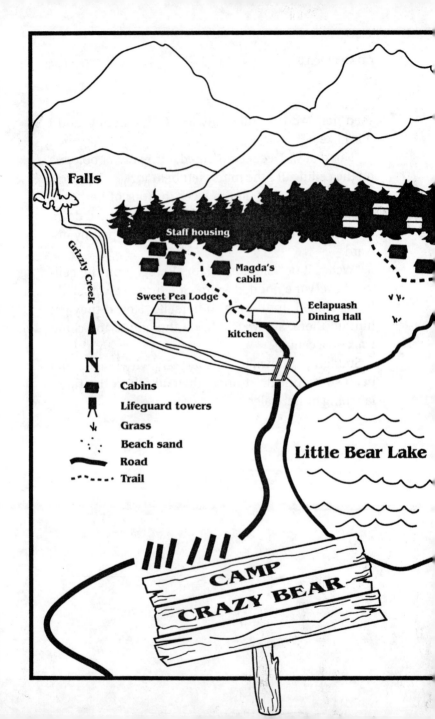

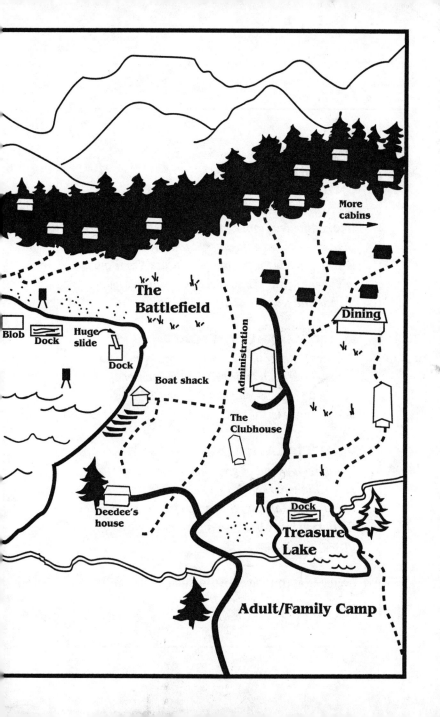

JOIN CHINA IN EACH UNFORGETTABLE ADVENTURE

Get ready for more action! Life in the United States is very different from what China is used to in Guatemala. She's enjoying her independence and is always ready for fun and adventure. Come along with her to Camp Crazy Bear as she makes new friends and learns important biblical truths.

SLICED HEATHER ON TOAST

Heather Hamilton, the snobby camp beauty, has it in for China from their very first encounter. It soon turns into a week-long war of practical jokes—and valuable lessons.

PROJECT BLACK BEAR

Thinking it would be great to have real bears for pets, China and Deedee set food out in an effort to lure the animals into the camp. But these are wild California black bears, and their plan causes an incredible disaster.

Available at your favorite Christian bookstore.